A NEW SADDLE CLUB PROJECT

There was a devious twinkle in Stevie's eye. "So, is everyone thinking what I'm thinking?"

"You mean about finding Max a wife?" Carole said.

"And that it's a perfect job for The Saddle Club?" Lisa chimed in.

"Exactly," Stevie replied. "But I'm already a step ahead of you guys. I was thinking about a certain annual event at Pine Hollow that would be the perfect opportunity to introduce Max to hundreds of eligible women."

"All I can think of is the Fourth of July picnic," Lisa said.

"That's it," Stevie answered. "It'll be up to The Saddle Club to bring in every single prospective wife we can think of. Then Max can choose one—with our advice, of course. . . ."

THE SADDLE CLUB

HAY FEVER

BONNIE BRYANT

BANTAM BOOKS
TORONTO · NEW YORK · LONDON · SYDNEY · AUCKLAND

THE SADDLE CLUB: HAY FEVER
A BANTAM BOOK 0 553 40763 5

First published in USA by Bantam Skylark Books
First publication in Great Britain

PRINTING HISTORY
Bantam edition published 1994

With thanks to Chris and Sam of Coltspring Riding School for
their help in the preparation of the cover

Bantam Books are published by Transworld Publishers Ltd,
61–63 Uxbridge Road, Ealing, London W5 5SA,
in Australia by Transworld Publishers (Australia) Pty Ltd,
15–25 Helles Avenue, Moorebank, NSW 2170,
and in New Zealand by Transworld Publishers (NZ) Ltd,
3 William Pickering Drive, Albany, Auckland.

Printed and bound in Great Britain by
Cox & Wyman Ltd, Reading, Berks.

*I would like to express my special thanks
to Caitlin C. Macy for her help
in the writing of this book.*

"WATCH OUT!" Carole Hanson called. She swerved Starlight to the side just in time to avoid a head-on collision with another horse and rider. "We're supposed to be trotting in a *clockwise* circle." She twisted around in the saddle to see who had almost run into her and met the familiar eyes of her friend Stevie Lake.

"That's not what Max told me," Stevie said. "He definitely said *counter*clockwise."

The two girls glanced around the outdoor ring. The other students in their afternoon lesson were trotting every which way. In the space of a few seconds, two more pairs almost collided. Angry shouts could be heard.

"Why on earth isn't Max doing something?" Stevie asked.

"I don't know, but I'm going to find out," replied Carole.

There was definitely something strange going on. Max Regnery, the manager of Pine Hollow Stables and the girls' instructor, always insisted on complete organization in his lessons. His strict discipline was one of the reasons that he was such a wonderful teacher. He was also smart, patient, and an excellent rider himself.

Carole and Stevie couldn't imagine taking lessons with anyone else. The two of them and their friend Lisa Atwood spent practically every waking moment at Pine Hollow or wishing they were there. They had even formed a group for people who loved horses and riding. It was called The Saddle Club, and all of its members had to be completely horse crazy, as well as willing to help each other out.

This time it looked as if Max needed The Saddle Club to help *him* out. Carole trotted quickly to the middle of the ring. Max was speaking with a redheaded woman she didn't recognize. He was explaining how to judge the correct distance apart for trotting poles. The redhead looked as if she was concentrating hard. Carole didn't want to interrupt, but the situation was getting out of hand fast.

"Uh, Max—" she began timidly. He ignored her.

"Excuse me, Max," she said more firmly. He still didn't seem to notice her.

"Max!" she fairly shouted.

The redhead spoke up. "Max, someone wants to talk to you."

Max looked up distractedly. "Yes, Deb? What are you doing in the middle of the ring?"

Taken aback, Carole paused for a second before correcting him. "It's Carole," she said. "And I was just wondering what direction we're supposed to be trotting in, because everyone's—"

"Yes," Max replied curtly, "you're supposed to be trotting. Now get back out there—heels down, okay, D— uh, Carole?" Turning back to the woman, Max sneezed several times.

Carole raised her eyebrows. Occasionally Max called her "Lisa" or "Stevie," mixing up the three girls because they spent so much time together. But *Deb?* Where'd that come from? And he *still* hadn't realized what was going on. "Max," she said, "I *know* we're supposed to be trotting. But in what *direction?*"

"Huh?"

The redhead interjected once again. "I think she's asking about the direction, Max," she said gently.

"Oh! Direction!" Max exclaimed, looking at the woman with admiration. "Clockwise, of course. Anything else?"

Carole shook her head weakly. All of a sudden she understood what people meant by the expression "talking to a wall." It was impossible to get through to Max today, and she had no idea why.

Carole quickly headed Starlight toward the far end of the ring, where Stevie and Lisa were walking side by side.

"Hey, that's a great new shirt, Stevie," Lisa was saying as Carole joined them.

"This? This isn't new," Stevie replied.

"Really? I've certainly never seen it before. Anyway, pink looks really good on you."

Carole listened impatiently for a minute, then decided that there were more important things to talk about than clothes. She hastily explained that Max was acting more out of it than she'd ever seen him. "He called me 'Deb,' or something like that twice, and that woman practically had to translate everything I asked him," she said.

Lisa frowned, glancing in the manager's direction. "That does *not* sound like Max."

"Who is that woman, anyway?" Stevie asked.

"I thought someone said she was a guest instructor," Lisa said.

"If she's a guest instructor, then Max has really flipped. She was just learning how to lay out trotting poles," Carole said. "Anyway, we're supposed to be going clock-wise, and I think we'd better spread the word before things get any crazier."

With that, Carole, Stevie, and Lisa turned Starlight, Topside, and Barq to go tell the others. Before they could get very far, however, Max summoned everyone into the center. When they had all gathered, he looked at the group nervously and cleared his throat several times. Finally he opened his mouth to speak—and ended up sneezing several times.

The Saddle Club looked at one another. "Is it my imagination, or is Max really nervous about something?" Lisa whispered.

"Nervous, for one, and it looks like he's sick, too," Stevie said under her breath.

"A few sneezes doesn't mean he's sick," Lisa whispered back.

"Who's talking about the sneezes?" Stevie asked. "He *must* be sick—he's not yelling at us for talking in class."

In spite of the situation, Lisa and Carole burst into giggles. Stevie always saw the funny side of everything. At school and at Pine Hollow her impish nature and love of practical jokes had gotten her into more scrapes than the three of them cared to remember. Luckily for The Saddle Club, she usually got herself right back out—often with surprisingly good results.

"Ahem." Max finally found his voice. "I have a question for the class. Did any of you see the front page of the *Washington Times* this morning?"

Lisa's hand shot up. A straight-A student, it was no surprise that Lisa would have read the newspaper. With typical modesty, however, she put her hand down quickly when she realized no one else had raised theirs. More than anything, Lisa hated to show off about her intelligence and good grades.

"I read the comics," Stevie volunteered eagerly. Everyone laughed, including the new woman.

"I'm glad to see you're challenging yourself, Stevie," Max replied drily. Carole grinned. That sounded more like the Max she knew.

"Well, Lisa, why don't you tell us if any particular story caught your eye."

Lisa thought hard for a minute. She remembered something about the President taking a trip, then there was some drought in California. . . . "Oh, I know!" she blurted out. "There was a big article on drugging racehorses at the track. Some man was arrested, and they said he'd been drugging practically his whole stable for years because no one could ever catch him. Most of the horses were supposed to have been retired because of stress injuries and strains, but the trainer kept drugging them up and racing them."

Max's approving smile told Lisa that she had given the right answer. "Exactly," he said, "only it wasn't a 'they' who said it. It was our very special guest at Pine Hollow this week, Miss Deborah Hale, news reporter extraordinaire." Max gestured toward the redheaded woman and then paused awkwardly. Having introduced the woman, he didn't seem to know what to do with himself. Deborah Hale, however, rose to the occasion.

"Oh, Max," she protested, "I was only doing my job."

"So does that mean you're investigating Pine Hollow for drugs, too?" Lisa asked.

"Yeah, I've noticed Topside's been a little sluggish, lately," Stevie kidded.

Max managed to give both of them the evil eye at once. "She most certainly is not doing anything of the kind." He explained that he had met Deborah a few weeks ago when she had first come to Willow Creek— the suburb of Washington, D.C., where they lived—to investigate.

"I needed to learn enough about horses—and fast—so that I wouldn't look suspicious around the track," Deborah said. Then she added, with a sidelong glance at Max, "Max is a wonderful teacher, as I'm sure you all know."

"So you don't even know how to ride?" a student standing in the back of the group asked condescendingly. In one motion the class turned to glare at the inquirer. Only one person at Pine Hollow could be that rude to a guest—Veronica diAngelo.

"Thank goodness she's leaving for her European vacation tomorrow," Lisa whispered.

"Europe's not far enough. She should go to Abu Dhabi," Stevie whispered back.

Veronica was an insensitive, spoiled girl whose purpose in life seemed to be making other people feel uncomfortable. Lisa, Carole, Stevie, and practically everyone else at Pine Hollow had long since given up on trying to be friends with her.

Deborah looked embarrassed at Veronica's remark. "No, I actually don't know how to ride. I'm hoping I'll learn quickly, though." She seemed to make a big effort to smile.

Meanwhile Max looked as if he was trying very hard to keep himself from exploding at Veronica. "All right, enough chatter," he barked. "Shorten your stirrups to jumping length, form a line, and start trotting over these cavalletti."

"But we haven't cantered yet or done any warm-up exercises on the flat," Lisa said, mystified. In all of her lessons at Pine Hollow, she had always been taught to warm up her horse thoroughly before jumping.

Max, who had turned to give Deborah an encouraging smile, flashed Lisa a dark look. "Well, what *have* you been doing for the past half hour?" he asked.

"Class only started ten minutes ago!" Lisa replied. Normally she wouldn't talk back to Max, but this was ridiculous!

Max looked down at his watch. "Oh, yeah," he said. "So it did." By this point the entire class—including the woman—was staring at Max, trying to figure out what strange disease had invaded his brain. He gave a sheepish grin. "Scratch that. Instead, pick up a sitting trot and prepare to canter."

The class looked at one another. No one moved. Even though he had finally given them some normal instructions, everyone seemed to be waiting for some signal that Max was really himself again. As if he knew what his students were thinking, Max spun on his heel and snapped, "What's everyone staring at? Don't the words 'sitting trot' mean anything to anyone? If not, I'd be happy to—ah—ah—AHCHOO!" With a resounding sneeze, Max cut himself short.

The Saddle Club and the others in the lesson picked up their reins and headed out to the rail. Obviously, whatever was wrong with Max was beyond their control —they would just have to get through the lesson and hope he didn't set up a six-foot fence for them to trot over!

"IF I HAD to go around one more time, I was going to quit riding and take up needlepoint—I'm sure it would be more interesting!" Stevie announced as she joined Lisa and Carole in the locker room after untacking. For the past half hour, Max had kept them trotting over the same ten poles while he demonstrated lengthening and shortening of stride to Deborah Hale.

"No kidding," Lisa agreed. "Max was on another planet."

9

"He certainly was acting strange," Carole said. "I know it was kind of funny—all his sneezing and being confused and everything—but do you think maybe something could be really wrong with him?"

"Gosh, I never even thought of that," Lisa admitted. "I'll bet it's probably just allergies, though—you know, hay fever or something."

Stevie's eyes opened wide. "Do you think so? What if he had pneumonia? Or bronchitis? Or mono?" she asked.

Lisa chose her words carefully. She knew that sickness was a very sensitive subject to Stevie these days since her brother Alex had been dangerously ill only a short time ago. Still, it was foolish to think a few sneezes meant that Max was really sick. "Look, if he were really sick, he wouldn't be up and about—not to mention teaching a lesson."

"That's true," Stevie said. She thought for a minute. "You know, I don't think Max has ever missed a day of teaching."

"We sure take him for granted, don't we?" Carole said. "Imagine if something ever did happen to him."

Stevie paused with one boot in the boot jack. Lisa looked up from combing her hair. Something happen to Max? Impossible—even to think about. Before they could freak each other out anymore, Carole took command of the situation. "All right, we're getting silly. I think this calls for a Saddle Club calm-down meeting at TD's. Okay?"

Lisa smiled in relief. "Sounds good," she said.

Stevie, however, looked less than pleased. "Maybe we should try somewhere else for a change," she muttered.

Lisa and Carole stared at her. Was Stevie starting to get weird now, too? The Saddle Club *always* went to TD's. Other than Pine Hollow, the local ice-cream shop was their main hangout.

"What do you mean 'somewhere else'?" Carole inquired cautiously.

"Nothing," Stevie mumbled. "It's just that I have a feeling my brother will be there with his date."

"So what's the big deal?" Carole asked. She knew Stevie wasn't too keen on socializing with her brothers, but she usually didn't worry about running into them in public places.

"Oh, I don't know. It's just that—"

"Hey!" Lisa exclaimed, interrupting suddenly. She pointed at Stevie's feet. "You *are* color coordinated today. Your pink socks match your shirt perfectly. You're getting interested in fashion, aren't you?" she asked.

Stevie sort of grumbled in response.

"I'll take that as a 'yes,' " Lisa said.

"And a 'yes' for TD's, too," Carole added.

Reluctantly Stevie nodded.

TWENTY MINUTES LATER The Saddle Club slid into their usual booth at TD's. The waitress's face lit up when she saw them come in. She came right over to take their order.

"A butterscotch sundae," Lisa decided.

"That sounds good—me too," Carole said.

"Have I got the perfect suggestion for you," the waitress said, looking at Stevie. "We're having a special on 'pinks'—bubble-gum ice cream, strawberry topping, maraschino cherries, and cinnamon sprinkles. You'll take it, right?"

Lisa and Carole smiled. It did sound like a perfect order for Stevie—perfectly disgusting, that is, like her usual concoctions. To their surprise Stevie shook her head. "No thank you, I'll skip the pinks," she said firmly. "I'll have blueberry ice cream, yellow pineapple topping, and rainbow sprinkles, please."

After the waitress left to place their order, Carole turned to Stevie.

"All right, what's up? You seem a little oversensitive to the word 'pink.'"

Stevie cringed. When her friends did some additional coaxing, she poured out the whole story. It had all begun when Stevie's mother, a busy lawyer, had gone on strike at home. She had announced at dinner the week before that she was tired of being everything to everyone and was going to insist that everyone pitch in.

"That doesn't sound so bad. I help my mom around the house sometimes," Lisa said.

"Yes, well, you haven't heard the whole thing," Stevie continued. "I got the job of doing the laundry. My red sweatshirt was in the first load, and it was really dirty, so I decided to wash it on the hottest temperature."

"Oh, no!" Lisa exclaimed. "Don't tell me you had other stuff in with it!"

Stevie nodded glumly. "Yeah. My white blouse, my white socks, my white underwear, and my *brothers'* white underwear."

"And red and white make pink," Carole finished for her, beginning to giggle. Lisa caught her eye, and in no time all three of them were struggling to stop laughing.

13

"It is pretty funny," Stevie admitted when she'd regained her composure. "But unfortunately my brothers don't see the humor in it. Pink is not exactly Alex, Chad, and Michael's favorite color. They're completely furious with me, and I think they're starting a campaign to kick me out of the house."

Lisa and Carole nodded sympathetically. They knew from past experience how tough the Lake brothers could be. Once, in front of Stevie's boyfriend, they had teased her about foxhunting so mercilessly that Stevie had had to wage an all-out war against them. Luckily she could usually hold her own. This time was no different.

"I guess if they do anything too terrible, I can always blackmail them into submission," Stevie said.

At the exact moment she made her pronouncement, Stevie's older brother Chad swung open the door to TD's, followed by the girl he'd been dating, a brunette named Amy. Stevie scrunched down in the booth, but Chad spotted her immediately.

"Well, well, well, if it isn't my darling sister, Stevie," he said, eyeing her coolly. "Hiding in the booth, huh? Hoping your friends will protect you?"

"Actually, Chad," Stevie said sweetly, "I was hoping I'd run into you here. I wanted to make sure you knew they were having a special on all-pink sundaes. And I know how much you *love* pink," she added.

Chad gave her a withering glance. "We'll continue

this discussion at home." He took the surprised Amy by the arm and propelled her through the door. "Come on," The Saddle Club girls heard him say as he exited, "we'll go somewhere less crowded."

"Well," Carole pointed out, "that could have been a lot worse."

"Yeah," Stevie muttered. "Try *living* with him—and the other two."

Lisa thought for a minute. "Have you tried bleaching the underwear? That should turn it white again," she suggested.

"That's what my mom told me," Stevie replied. "But then I remembered that I stole the bleach last month and took it to Pine Hollow to treat the new pony's thrush."

"Can't you buy some more?" Lisa asked logically.

Stevie looked at her in surprise. "Are you suggesting that I spend my hard-earned money on my *brothers*?" she asked.

Carole and Lisa looked at one another. When it came to her brothers, Stevie could be completely irrational.

While they talked, the waitress had appeared from behind the counter with a trayful of sundaes. She set the first two down in front of Carole and Lisa. Then she gingerly picked up the blueberry-pineapple dish, examined it briefly, wrinkled up her nose, and pushed it toward Stevie with distaste. "Waste of good ice cream, if you ask me," she muttered.

"Speaking of ice cream," Stevie piped up, "I'd better have something else to go with this. How 'bout a nice, normal brownie sundae?"

"On top of what you've got?" the waitress demanded.

"Naturally. This is the appetizer. That's the main course," Stevie replied. Shaking her head, the waitress went to place the order.

"I figured I'd better eat up," Stevie explained. "I just remembered it's Chad's night to cook, and I don't want to face it on an empty stomach."

"Good idea," Carole agreed.

After a few minutes of silent spooning, the girls set about the business at hand: figuring out Max's strange behavior at the lesson.

"Maybe he's got Alzheimer's," Stevie suggested. "I think my great-uncle had it, and he could never remember anything."

"Alzheimer's? Please, Stevie, Max is way too young to get that," Lisa admonished.

"Well, I didn't know," Stevie said defensively. "And, anyway, Max isn't exactly a spring chicken. I think I heard Mrs. Reg say that he's almost thirty."

"Thirty?" Carole repeated. "Wow, that's practically ancient."

"Yeah, and he's still single," Lisa pointed out.

"I wonder if he's ever had a girlfriend," Stevie mused. She grinned as she remembered the time not too long ago when the three of them had jumped to conclusions about Max's love life. They'd overheard him talking on the phone, and thought he had a girlfriend—when in fact he'd been talking about a new mare for Pine Hollow!

Before she could remind her friends of the last time they'd gotten involved in Max's love life, Lisa clapped her hands together. "Stevie, that's probably it!" she said.

"What's it?"

"Maybe Deborah Hale is Max's new girlfriend! That would explain his acting weird and forgetting stuff. He might have been nervous around her," Lisa said.

Stevie and Carole thought over Lisa's explanation. "I just can't believe that Max would be interested in someone like her," Carole finally said. "She doesn't ride, for one."

"So? I like Bob Harris, and he doesn't ride. He plays soccer," Lisa replied. Bob Harris was a school friend of Stevie's whom Lisa had really hit it off with at Carole's birthday party.

"That's true, but I don't think she's his type in other ways, too. She seemed nice but too sensitive," Stevie said. "I'd guess Max would like a woman with a strong personality like his. And I'm beginning to think that he was simply nervous about having a reporter around while he tried to teach a lesson. She's probably the type who's

17

always taking mental notes on everything. That can get to you after a while—not knowing if what you say will end up in tomorrow's front page." Stevie gave Lisa a significant glance. Once Lisa had tried writing a column for the local newspaper. The only problem had been that it had unknowingly turned her into a snoop and a tattle-tale on her friends.

"Okay, okay," Lisa conceded. "I see what you mean."

After a minute Carole said thoughtfully, "Still, it does seem kind of sad that Max is thirty and he doesn't even have a girlfriend, let alone a wife. He's probably lonely."

"Yeah, and if he doesn't get married soon, there might never be an heir to take over Pine Hollow. And then what would our kids do for a riding instructor?" Stevie asked.

It was a cherished dream among The Saddle Club that their children—who would naturally be horse-crazy girls, as they were—would learn to ride at Pine Hollow, just as they had. If Max weren't around to teach them, then it was only fitting that Max the Fourth do the job. The current Max Regnery—*their* Max Regnery—was the third Max to own and operate Pine Hollow. Naturally, the girls wanted to ensure that there would be a Max the Fourth to succeed him at the stable.

"One thing's for sure, you can't have a Max the Fourth without a Mrs. Max," Lisa said.

"Don't forget," Stevie pointed out, "there's always the chance that he would only have daughters."

"That's okay," Lisa replied, smiling. "Maxine the Fourth would be just fine. Maybe even better."

They all laughed.

There was a devious twinkle in Stevie's eye. "So is everyone thinking what I'm thinking?"

"You mean about finding Max a wife?" Carole said.

"And that it's a perfect job for The Saddle Club?" Lisa chimed in.

"Exactly," Stevie replied. "But I'm a step ahead of you guys. I was thinking about a certain annual event at Pine Hollow that would be the perfect opportunity to introduce Max to hundreds of eligible women."

Lisa and Carole thought for a minute. Hundreds of eligible women? Stevie obviously knew something they didn't. The only summer event coming up was the Fourth of July picnic next weekend. Every year all the students, parents, employees, and friends of Pine Hollow gathered at the stables for a day of horses, socializing, and barbecuing. But it wasn't as if attractive women in their twenties and thirties flocked to the party!

"I give up," Lisa said. "All I can think of is the picnic."

"Same," Carole said.

"That's it!" Stevie cried. "The Fourth of July picnic."

"But it's not the type of thing that draws single

women," Carole commented drily. "Usually it's just the riders and some of the parents."

"Don't you see?" Stevie answered. "That's where *we* come in. It'll be up to The Saddle Club to bring in every single prospective wife we can think of. Then Max can choose one—with our advice, of course."

Carole and Lisa nodded. It hadn't occurred to them that Max might pick out some completely unsuitable bride, but it *was* a possibility. And they all knew from being around horses how important good bloodlines, temperament, and conformation were in breeding the perfect offspring. If Max found some undesirable woman and married her, The Saddle Club would be stuck with her and her progeny for as long as they—not to mention their children—rode at Pine Hollow.

"Good thing we're getting involved now," Carole said.

"Without us Max might find some awful woman to marry—or forget about marriage altogether," Lisa said.

"I'm sure he'll thank us at the end," Stevie predicted. She whipped a stub of a pencil out of her jeans pocket and began to scrawl on a napkin. After a few minutes she pushed the napkin toward Carole and Lisa. "Anything I should add?" she asked.

They looked at the list. It read: *Mrs. Max must be: (1) horsey (or at least very interested in learning about horses), (2) friendly, especially toward Max's students, (3) interested in helping Max out around the barn, (4) in good health, (5) smart, (6) beautiful.*

"Sounds perfect to me," Carole said.

"That definitely sums up the perfect wife for him," Lisa agreed. "I just hope we'll meet some women who fit the description."

"Don't worry—there'll be tons of them," Stevie assured her confidently. "Oh, good, here's dinner." She licked her lips with anticipation as the waitress set a huge brownie sundae down in front of her.

"If you were my kid and ate that for dinner, I'd take away your allowance," the waitress announced.

"Yeah, well, you see, my mom—" Stevie began. Then she stopped suddenly and stared at the waitress. She was tall, lanky, had good balance (from carrying trays of sundaes), and a healthy glow to her skin. Friendly, they could work on. Putting a super-friendly smile on her face, she looked up at the waitress sweetly. "Would you mind turning around?" she asked.

The waitress looked surprised at the sudden change in subject. "What is this? Some kinda mind game?" she asked suspiciously.

Stevie shook her head. "Oh, no. What I meant to ask you was, are you married?"

"What's it to you?" the waitress shot back.

"Do you like to ride horses?" she asked.

"Are you giving me the third degree?" the waitress

21

asked. "Sure, I like to ride. I've only been twice in my life, though."

"Oh, that's okay," Stevie said. She made an effort to make her voice sound casual. "So how would you like to come to a nice, old-fashioned Fourth of July picnic at the stables where we ride?"

The waitress laughed. "Thanks for the offer, but I've got to work. That's one of our biggest days here."

Stevie's face fell. "Oh, well." She sighed. "Back to the drawing board."

The waitress gave her a funny look, left the check on the table, and turned to go back to the counter. Watching her walk away, Stevie sighed again. "Too bad. I have a feeling Max would appreciate her sense of humor."

NORMALLY LISA BARELY noticed when her mother invited friends or co-workers over for dinner. Mrs. Atwood worked part-time at the local mall as a hand model. That meant when the salesmen needed a picture of a salad on a plate, Mrs. Atwood's hands would be the ones pouring the dressing onto the lettuce—or stirring the stew or putting a casserole into the oven. A couple of times she had brought a lonely food photographer or kitchen-wares salesman home for a good, hot meal.

But tonight, when Lisa sat down at the table for dinner opposite the guest, her jaw dropped.

"Lisa, dear, this is Tiffani, one of the new models at Paris Chic."

In a daze Lisa held her hand out to shake with Tiffani.

Paris Chic was the most expensive clothing store in Willow Creek, known for its stylish dresses and suits, which were all imported from France.

"It's Tiffani with an *i*," the model said. Lisa nodded and stared. The woman was tall, slim, and gorgeous. She had the sleekest, straightest blond hair Lisa could imagine, and huge green eyes.

"How old are you?" Lisa blurted out.

"Lisa!" Mrs. Atwood reprimanded her. "That's not a very polite question."

Lisa glanced at Tiffani. "Sorry," she said.

Tiffani giggled. When she smiled, her lips parted to reveal a perfect row of pearly whites. "That's okay," she said. "I'm twenty-three."

"Perfect!" Lisa cried.

Mrs. Atwood gave her a shocked glance.

"I mean, uh, that must be a perfect age for enjoying a lot of things," Lisa explained lamely.

Tiffani giggled again. "It sure is, Lisa," she said.

The phone rang and Mrs. Atwood went to answer it. "It's probably your father," she said to Lisa. "He's working late tonight."

While her mother was out of the room, Lisa decided to risk a couple more questions. "Do you have to exercise a lot to keep yourself so thin?" she asked.

"All the time," Tiffani said. "Some people think modeling is really easy, but it's actually hard work."

Lisa nodded. She knew all about that. Once she and Stevie had been selected to "model" for a tack-shop catalog. They had been incredibly excited. But it turned out all they got to do was stand around for hours at a time, moving saddles, bridles, and horses for the photographer. It had ended up being a tiring and boring day. From the looks of her, though, Tiffani probably got to do more glamorous jobs than they had.

"Do you ever go riding?" Lisa asked.

"You mean for exercise? Not really. I usually run or do aerobics," Tiffani said. "But once I did a commercial for Windswept perfume, and I had to ride a horse across a field." She giggled. "It was fun."

Lisa wasted no time. Her mother would be back in a second. "You could go again with me sometime. I ride at Pine Hollow Stables. Come to think of it, there's the Fourth of July picnic coming up. That would be the perfect time for you to come. And did I mention Pine Hollow's *wonderful* owner? His name's Max, and he's really smart and good-looking and—" Lisa stopped abruptly as she heard her mother hang up the phone.

Tiffani giggled. "Sounds fun. Count me in," she said.

Lisa smiled and said nothing.

"I hope you're both hungry," Mrs. Atwood said, reentering the room with a huge dish of lasagna.

"Sure am, Mom," Lisa said with a grin. She could hardly believe her luck. She'd hardly even started to look, and already she had a beautiful candidate for Max. Beautiful and friendly and—well, you couldn't have everything.

"Has it started yet?" Carole's father called from the kitchen.

"No, we've still got at least five minutes of commercials," Carole called back. She and her father were planning to eat dinner in front of the TV so they could watch the movie *The Longest Day* together. They had set up card tables to hold the plates of food, and Colonel Hanson was getting out ketchup, mustard, and pickles for the bacon cheeseburgers he had made.

Carole's mother had died a few years ago, and she was very close to her father. Watching old movies—especially war movies—was a tradition in the Hanson household.

"*Bon appétit,*" Colonel Hanson said as he brought in the condiments.

"Yum," Carole said. "These look like they could become your new specialty, Dad."

"Better than microwave pizza?" Colonel Hanson queried.

Carole took a big bite out of her burger. "Absolutely," she said.

Eating dinner with her father reminded her of The

Saddle Club matter at hand. "Dad, would you say an ability to cook is a must in a possible wife?" she inquired.

Colonel Hanson looked suspicious. "Why?" he asked. Ever since Carole's mother had died, well-meaning but meddlesome people had been trying to set him up with women.

Carole reassured her father. "Don't worry, Dad. It's got nothing to do with you. It's just that Lisa and Stevie and I realized today that Max is very lonely. Not only that, he's getting kind of old, and unless he gets married and has children soon, he might never find a wife. Then our children wouldn't be able to take lessons with his heir—Max the Fourth—and they'd have to learn to ride from a total stranger, so we decided to find him a wife, and we made up a list of attributes she had to have, and I was just thinking maybe we should have put 'cooking skill' on the list."

Colonel Hanson laughed. "Boy, you're pretty worked up about this, aren't you?"

"Dad, it's not funny. We're serious about this. The future of Pine Hollow is at stake."

Colonel Hanson paused, chewing thoughtfully. Carole waited eagerly for his response. She was positive that he would be on their side.

Finally he spoke. "It's not that I think your trying to help Max is funny, Carole. But you have to remember that there are some things a person has to do for himself.

27

For example, people are always pushing unmarried women at me. And the only one I'm interested in is someone I met on my own, right?"

Carole nodded. Her father had been dating Mrs. Dana for several months. And he had decided all on his own to ask Mrs. Dana out on a date. But wait a minute, Carole thought. First, I became friends with Mrs. Dana's daughter. That's how Dad and Mrs. Dana met.

Without Carole's help, both her father and Mrs. Dana would still be putting up with blind dates. Her father might think he'd done it on his own, but Carole knew otherwise. She'd been directly involved.

Colonel Hanson turned toward the TV. The theme song to the movie had just begun.

"Thanks, Dad," Carole said, patting him on the arm.

Colonel Hanson beamed. "Anytime," he replied. "Imparting wisdom is part of my job as your father."

Carole grinned and settled in to watch the movie.

At the first commercial break, Colonel Hanson turned back toward his daughter. "Do all these soldiers remind you of anything?"

"I don't think so," Carole replied.

Colonel Hanson pretended to swoon. "I'm crushed, but I hope you'll still be able to find time to come to the base tomorrow. Remember? It's 'Take Your Daughter to Quantico Day.' "

"Oh, Dad, now I remember! Of course. You said that

everyone in the battalion is invited to bring his or her daughter to work to see what their parents do all day. I can't wait."

"Even if it cuts into your riding time?" Colonel Hanson asked. He knew that Carole could have a one-track mind about how to spend the day, every day.

"I'm sure Starlight will understand," Carole said. "I'll just tell him that the Marine Corps needs me," she joked.

"That's right, ma'am," Colonel Hanson replied, saluting smartly. "We're always looking for a few good women."

"Yes, sir!"

THE TINKLE OF the dinner bell called the Lake family to the table. When the five of them—minus Chad who was putting the finishing touches on his gourmet dinner—had sat down, Stevie looked piteously across the table at her brothers. A few minutes before, her twin Alex and her little brother Michael had announced that they were both starving and could hardly wait to see what Chad had whipped up. Poor souls, Stevie thought. If only they'd had the presence of mind to eat a brownie sundae an hour ago. She was hardly hungry at all now, and she figured it would be easy enough to push the food around on her plate and avoid actually eating any of it.

"Smells good, Chad," Mrs. Lake called encouragingly.

She looked happy and refreshed, having relaxed with the newspaper and a glass of wine, instead of cooking dinner.

Stevie glanced at her mother, wondering if she'd thought to grab a burger on her way home from the law firm.

"Dinner is served," Chad announced. He walked into the dining room carrying a tray laden with serving bowls.

Stevie closed her eyes and prepared for the worst. She opened them just as Chad was whisking the covers off the dishes. For a minute Stevie thought her eyes still hadn't adjusted to the light. All the food looked purple.

Chad grinned wickedly at her. "*Some* of us have gotten a little tired of the color pink lately," he said. "I decided it might be nice to have dinner in a different color. So help yourselves."

Stevie had been right. The food really *was* purple. There was what looked like fettuccine Alfredo dyed purple with food coloring, a purple cabbage and purple onion salad, and grape juice to drink.

Stevie looked around the table. Her mother and father and brothers all looked as if they were about to burst out laughing. Stevie beat them to it. She laughed so hard her face started to turn the color of the meal. The rest of the Lakes joined in, including Chad, the triumphant cook. Stevie had to hand it to her brother—he could be very clever when he wanted to be. She, for one, was impressed.

"You know what the really funny thing about this purple food is?" Stevie asked when she could breathe again. She stuffed a bite of pasta into her mouth. "It's really good!"

Right after dinner—as soon as she had pitched in with clearing and washing dishes—Stevie dashed up to her room. She wanted to call Carole and Lisa to tell them how dinner had turned out. Lisa's line was busy, so she tried Carole. Carole laughed when Stevie told her the story, but she sounded distracted.

"What's up?" Stevie asked. "It sounds like you're in two places at once."

"You're right," Carole admitted. "I keep thinking about the Max problem."

"Problem? It's not a problem yet, Carole. We've only just begun."

"I know, but the Fourth is only days away," Carole pointed out.

"I think it'll be fun to find women for Max to marry—I mean *a* woman. The candidates will probably all be really nice to get to know," Stevie said.

"You know, you're right," Carole answered. "My father has met a ton of women over the last year, and some of them *were* pretty nice."

"Why didn't we think of that earlier? You could get all of their names out of your dad's address file and invite them to the picnic," Stevie suggested.

"That's true, but—"

"Don't worry: I'm sure they'd remember who you are. Didn't you say they were always trying to get on your good side?"

Carole smiled into the receiver. In her enthusiasm Stevie had forgotten one important point. "Sure, that's a great idea," Carole said, "as long as Max doesn't mind dating women fifteen years older than he is!"

Stevie realized her mistake. It was really too bad—Colonel Hanson's files would have been such a great resource. Maybe there was still some way they could use them. Love could cross age barriers, couldn't it? "Hey, what's a generation or two when you're in love?" she said.

"Nothing," Carole teased. "That's why you can't wait to meet a nice, handsome twenty-eight-year-old, right?"

Stevie laughed. "Okay, okay. I get the point. But at least we'll have some backups if we can't find some younger women," she added.

LISA RAN BREATHLESSLY into the stable at Pine Hollow the next morning. She was practically bursting with the news about Tiffani and couldn't wait to tell Carole and Stevie about her "model" candidate. She had tried to reach them the night before, but both lines had stayed busy for an hour—no doubt talking to one another, Lisa guessed. Luckily, The Saddle Club had planned to meet at ten A.M. to go riding together.

"Carole! Stevie!" Lisa called.

"Hi, Lisa! I'm over here!" Carole answered. Lisa didn't have to ask where "over here" was. Carole's voice came from the direction of Starlight's stall. Besides, Lisa knew from experience that nine times out of ten she could find Carole there. Before she'd owned her own horse, Carole

33

had spent hours fussing over whomever she was riding. Now that Starlight was hers, she spent decades!

Sure enough, Carole had the bay gelding cross-tied in front of his stall and was currying him vigorously.

"Is Stevie here yet?" Lisa asked. "I have some news."

"No, I haven't seen her. I guess she's running late. She told me she wanted to get here early and lunge Topside before riding. He's in such good shape that he's been too full of energy lately." Topside was the former show horse that Stevie always rode.

Lisa was going to wait to share her news until Stevie came, but she just couldn't. "Guess what? I found a model for Max!" she told Carole. She described Tiffani's looks in great detail—her perfect teeth, her long blond hair, and her huge green eyes. "So I invited her to the picnic, and she's going to come," Lisa finished happily.

"And what's she like?" Carole asked.

"What do you mean?" Lisa countered.

"Well, I mean what's her personality like?"

"Oh. Oh, she's—uh—friendly, very friendly. Yes, I'd definitely say friendly. It was a little hard to talk to her, but I guess that's because she's older. She really didn't have much to say. And she looked at her nails a lot. But she's absolutely gorgeous."

"That's nice," Carole said a touch uneasily.

"Nice? It's great!" Lisa said. She wondered if Carole realized what an opportunity this was.

"Yeah, I mean, that's great," Carole said. She paused for a minute, figuring out how to continue. "It's great," she said finally, "but remember what kind of a guy Max is. He might rather have a smart wife—who's also pretty —than a drop-dead gorgeous one. Tiffani sounds, well, a tiny bit dense."

To Carole's relief Lisa laughed heartily. "Dense? She seemed dumber than a doornail to me. All she did was giggle and look beautiful. But I thought Max wouldn't mind since they could have such beautiful children."

"Beautiful maybe, but they've also got to have the sense to operate Pine Hollow, and that's no easy job—as we should know!" Carole responded. She was referring to The Saddle Club's attempt, several months earlier, to run Pine Hollow while Max was away.

Lisa had to agree. "We certainly got into a million mishaps, even with our great brains," she said.

"Speaking of mishaps, what do you think has become of Stevie?" Carole asked. "I'm really surprised she hasn't shown up by now."

Lisa glanced at her watch. "I say we give her another half an hour to call. I hope we won't have to go without her. It's such a beautiful day for riding."

STEVIE SWUNG HER leg back and then forward as she kicked the groaning, whirring machine as hard as she could. "Stupid vacuum cleaner!" she yelled. Unfortunately, the attack backfired. After making contact with the vacuum, Stevie recoiled her foot in pain while the vacuum stayed obstinately in place.

Life, Stevie decided, had never been more unfair. Or at least her mother hadn't. Here it was, a beautiful summer day, at the beginning of a beautiful school vacation. The whole school year long she had looked forward to—no, *dreamed* of—days like this when she would sleep late, then go over to Pine Hollow to enjoy riding and hanging out with Lisa and Carole to her heart's content. Mrs. Lake, however, had had other ideas. She had quickly put an end to the bliss of a lazy summer vacation with her insistence that Stevie and her brothers pitch in around the house. Today Stevie was not allowed to leave until all the vacuuming was done. It was worse than homework—at least with homework you could skim assignments and fudge problems. If you skimped on housework, everyone knew.

Sighing loudly, Stevie flopped down on the couch for a break. She stared at the clock on the wall, willing the hands not to move. Her mind wandered to all the things she was missing. She'd already missed meeting with Lisa and Carole for a long, gossipy chat about the Max situation. Right about now she was missing grooming and tacking up with them. And unless she finished the rugs pretty soon, she was going to miss their ride together and cleaning tack afterward. Of course, she'd have to do all those things later, when she finally got to Pine Hollow, but they would be far less enjoyable alone—especially the barn chores.

After a few minutes of brooding, Stevie forced herself to get to her feet again, turn the machine on, and continue vacuuming. Idly she pushed the heavy nozzle back and forth, still thinking about how ruined her day was. She was so preoccupied with her Saddle Club thoughts that she hardly noticed when the vacuum sucked up her father's favorite pen.

"Oh, no!" Stevie groaned aloud. One minute the gold fountain pen had been there, the next it was gone. Why hadn't she picked it up the second she saw it? It wasn't only valuable—it was also a sentimental favorite, because Mr. Lake's partners at the office had given it to him on his tenth anniversary of working there. Stevie shook her head ruefully. The only thing to do—if she valued her life—was to make sure it didn't stay sucked up for good.

First she detached the bag from the hose and peered all the way up the hose. She couldn't see anything. Then she reached her hand up. She couldn't feel anything either. She spied an iron skewer over by the fireplace used to poke wood, grabbed it, and poked that up the hose. Nothing—except that she managed to poke a hole in the hose, which she would now have to find a way to fix. Finally she banged the hose on the coffee table, hoping to dislodge the pen from wherever it was stuck. A mess of hair and junk rained down on the table. But no pen appeared.

Stevie was about to give the vacuum another kick when the phone rang. "I'll be back," she muttered threateningly to the Electro-Clean, and went to pick up the receiver.

"Hello, Stephanie," the voice said. Stevie would recognize that cheery voice anywhere. It was Miss Cartwright, her science teacher.

"I've just been looking through my files, and I realized that I don't have your final project. Of course I can't give you a grade without it, and report cards were due last week. So you have an Incomplete in science for the moment, which I'll change to a grade as soon as I get the project."

Stevie could hardly trust herself to speak. If she did, she thought she would either cry or, more likely, scream at the top of her lungs. Obviously this was *not* her day. She was positive she had done the project. Distinct memories of wilted, dry, and dying leaves of the plants she had tried to grow came back to her in a flash. She had been trying to see how different types of soil affected the rate of growth of red, white, and blue blossoms. Unfortunately, the one thing she had discovered for sure was that plants die without water: She had forgotten to water them for about two weeks. Nevertheless, she was sure she could figure out some explanation for the teacher.

"Miss Cartwright," Stevie began, after calming herself with a deep breath, "I know I have the project. In fact, I even know where it is. It's upstairs in my bedroom closet."

"So you're sure you can find it?" Miss Cartwright asked.

Stevie tried to picture where in her closet the cardboard graphs charting the plants' growth would be. Under about a ton of dirty clothes, shoes, boxes of school papers, stuffed animals, photo albums, and random horsey stuff, she decided. It could take a little while to actually lay her hands on it—like maybe a millennium. Anyway, Miss Cartwright was one of the nicer teachers at Fenton Hall. She was young and pretty—not like some of the mean ones who'd been there for thirty years. If Stevie told her she could find it in a week or so, she probably wouldn't mind.

"Miss Cartwright?" Stevie began in the sweetest, most innocent tone she could manage. All at once her brain did a double take. Miss Cartwright? Nice? Young? Pretty? The phone call had suddenly turned into a golden Saddle Club opportunity. And what was more, Stevie had the perfect lead-in.

"Remember how the flowers I was growing were supposed to be red, white, and blue?" she asked. "Well, I was hoping to have them all blooming by the Fourth of July."

"I see," Miss Cartwright replied. "So what you're saying is that you won't be handing it in until next weekend?"

"Right," Stevie said.

"All right, then. Why don't you just drop it by my house, okay?"

"Actually," Stevie said all in a rush, "I thought you might want to come to the annual Fourth of July picnic at Pine Hollow Stables where my friends and I ride. It's always a great day—games, food, you know—and I could give you the project then, too." Stevie crossed her fingers. If she could have a whole week to find her project and also get another eligible woman to come to the picnic, this day might not be so bad after all.

"That's awfully kind of you, Stevie," Miss Cartwright said, "but I'm afraid my younger sisters will be visiting me for the weekend. I do appreciate the invitation, though. You know I used to ride when I was younger? Of course I haven't been on a horse in years, but I'll bet some of it would come back."

It took Stevie a minute to recover her composure. Could she have heard correctly—younger sisters? "How old are your sisters?" she asked, trying to sound nonchalant.

Miss Cartwright laughed. She was used to having

Stevie cut right to the point. "Actually, they're both twenty-three. They're twins."

"But that's even better!" Stevie blurted out. "I mean, uh, it would be great if you came and brought them, too." Twins? Stevie thought. This was getting exciting.

"Really? I'm sure they'd love to. Won't it be too many people, then?"

"Oh, *no*, Miss Cartwright. The more, the merrier. That's what Max Regnery, the owner of Pine Hollow, always says. He's so friendly—he just loves to meet new people. I can't wait to introduce him to you and your sisters. I'm sure you'll think he's wonderful."

"I'm sure we will, Stevie. Thank you for inviting us."

"Thank *you* for coming, Miss Cartwright." Stevie was about to hang up in a haze of well-being when Miss Cartwright's final words interrupted her reverie.

"I'll look forward to seeing your project then, too," she said. "Good-bye."

"Oh, right," Stevie muttered as the dial tone sounded in her ear. Anyway, digging out her science project would be a small price to pay for finding Max a suitable wife. After all, her children would be thanking her all their lives for sending them to Pine Hollow to ride with Max the Fourth.

Thinking of Pine Hollow gave Stevie new motivation to finish vacuuming and get over there. She could hardly wait to tell Carole and Lisa to add three more women to the list of potential mates. But first she absolutely had to find her father's gold pen.

In a flash of inspiration, she removed the vacuum bag from the machine and dumped everything out onto the carpet. She squatted down on the floor to begin examining the mess. Then she saw the telltale flash of gold. The pen was lying under the couch, just within reach and perfectly safe. It hadn't gotten sucked up at all.

Stevie looked from it to the pile of dirt and dust on the carpet that represented the morning's vacuuming. She didn't know whether to laugh or cry. Finally she lay down on the couch and laughed until her stomach ached.

BEFORE LEAVING FOR Pine Hollow later that morning, Stevie decided to conduct a quick search of her closet for her science project. As she expected, the cardboard graph was there—halfway filled out—but none of the pots were in sight. Stevie began to panic. How could she start over now? The Fourth was a week away; nothing would grow that fast. Moreover, Miss Cartwright was not only one of the nicest teachers at Fenton Hall, she was also one of the toughest. Rather than let Stevie take a failing grade, she would probably make her do the whole thing over just to get a passing D. Meanwhile the perfect day was slipping away.

Stevie made a characteristic split-second decision: She would go to Pine Hollow now, come up with a plan later.

In a flash she grabbed her stuff and headed for the door. Before she could close it, the phone rang. Stevie groaned. At this rate she would never catch Lisa and Carole. She ran to pick up the receiver. It was Mrs. Lake calling on her lunch break to see how the vacuuming was going.

"Great," Stevie told her, "now that it's done." Actually, the house did look great. Every speck of dust had vanished.

"Housework's like that," Mrs. Lake answered.

"Say, Mom, speaking of housework, I was cleaning out my closet today, and I was just wondering—you don't happen to know what happened to those three pots of plants I was growing for science, do you?"

"Oh, you mean the three pots of dead weeds? Sure. I found them drying up underneath your bed, so I watered them and relocated them to the back porch. They're looking great now, especially the red ones. I think the soil they're in may be better than the white and blue flowers' soil."

Stevie squealed with joy. Never mind getting a D— this looked like an A project. "You're the best!" she shouted.

"Gee, I didn't know vacuuming would have such a marvelous effect on you. I hope dusting is as fun," Mrs. Lake said.

"Thanks again, Mom," Stevie said.

"Anytime. I'll see you tonight for your father's dinner," she added.

After hanging up Stevie raced to the back porch. There, in the row of houseplants that her mother moved outside during the summer, were three pots of flowers, overflowing with red, white, and blue blossoms.

"Yippee!" Stevie kicked up her heels and took off for Pine Hollow. Hurrying over, she hoped that she would catch Lisa and Carole to share the news.

Both of her friends looked up from cleaning their tack when Stevie walked in ten minutes later.

"What happened?" Carole asked. "You missed a great outdoor schooling session."

Stevie groaned. "I know, I know. And I'm sure you're all done grooming and are just finishing up your tack."

Lisa and Carole nodded truthfully.

"Unfortunately, housework now takes precedence over horses at my house," Stevie said. She related her morning trials to them. Lisa and Carole commiserated, like the good friends they were.

"But if you can believe it, I have good news, too," Stevie said.

"Your mom decided you did such a good job that you don't have to help anymore?" Lisa guessed hopefully.

"Fat chance," Stevie said. "When she sees the rugs, she'll probably want me to quit school and be a full time housedaughter.

"The good news is that while I was vacuuming, Miss Cartwright, my science teacher, called and said that she didn't have my final science project so I have an Incomplete until she sees it."

"That's *good* news?" asked Lisa. With perfect grades since first grade, Lisa couldn't imagine why on earth Stevie would appreciate having an Incomplete on her report card.

"Let me finish," Stevie protested. She explained the coincidence of her project's red, white, and blue flowers and the Fourth of July picnic and Miss Cartwright's twin sisters' visit and her mother's rescue of the plants.

"You'll probably get an A," Lisa predicted.

"That'd be nice for a change," Stevie said.

"And all three sisters are coming?" Carole asked incredulously.

"All three of them," Stevie said. "And Miss Cartwright said she used to ride when she was little."

"Then that makes a total of four candidates for Mrs. Max so far," Lisa said. She told Stevie about Tiffani. "I'm not positive that she's smart enough for Max, but we at least have to give him the option of choosing someone who's totally beautiful."

As Carole was trying to absorb all this information, a horn tooted in the driveway—unmistakably her father's jeep. She gave a quick last swipe to her saddle and placed it carefully back on its rack.

"Gotta run, guys," she said, gathering up her stuff.

"You're leaving now?" Stevie asked. Even though Carole had said that she was almost finished with her tack, that didn't mean she wouldn't hang out at Pine Hollow for hours, grooming and regrooming Starlight and finding work to do around the barn. In fact, Stevie had been counting on her for company while she tacked up. She told Carole so.

"I guess Lisa will just have to keep you and Topside company," Carole replied. "Today is 'Bring Your Daughter to Work Day' at Quantico, and Dad is going to show me around so I can see what he does all day."

Lisa and Stevie thought it sounded like a great idea.

"I wonder if you'll see any top-secret maneuvers," Stevie said. "Like in *The Sands of Iwo Jima.*"

Carole laughed tolerantly. She was used to civilians thinking that military life was just like the movies— especially Stevie, who, like Colonel Hanson, had a passion for films from the fifties, many of which seemed to be set during World War II.

"I think it'll probably be pretty routine stuff," Carole said. As she headed for the driveway, she paused at the stable door and called back over her shoulder, "If we play any war games, I'll be sure to remember them for our next Pony Club mounted-games meeting!"

"Good idea!" Lisa yelled. "I'm sure Stevie wouldn't

want to miss an opportunity to attack Phil on horse-back!"

Phil Marsten was Stevie's boyfriend. He belonged to Cross County Pony Club. The Saddle Club all belonged to the Horse Wise club, which met at Pine Hollow. The two clubs often competed against one another—in rallies, Know-downs, and mounted games. Stevie and Phil were known for being almost as fond of competition as they were of each other.

"You'd better believe it," Stevie said, in response to Lisa's comment.

Colonel Hanson waved hello from the jeep as soon as Carole came outside to meet him.

"Hello, daughter," he said, saluting her formally through the window. He was wearing the green-on-khaki uniform he always wore for routine days on base.

"So, Dad," Carole said, climbing up to join him in the jeep, "will I be seeing any super-important, classified action today?"

Colonel Hanson chuckled. "Sorry, honey, but how about lunch at the Officers' Club to start with?"

"Sounds great," Carole said. As usual, she had worked up a huge appetite while riding. "And *then* we'll take care of the bloodless revolutions in the halls of Montezuma, right?"

"I don't know—I thought we might have to battle on the shores of Tripoli, actually," Colonel Hanson replied.

"Well, naturally," Carole said. They passed the rest of the ride kidding each other.

Even though Carole laughed and joked, half of her mind was somewhere else—back at Pine Hollow, where it usually was, with Stevie and Lisa. Carole felt that she was really letting them down, not to mention Max, because she hadn't been able to think of even one woman to invite to the picnic. She had even looked through her father's address book to make sure that all of the women really were too old for Max.

What if Max didn't find anyone he liked? He was sure to become depressed and, sooner or later, desperate for a wife. For all she knew, he felt that way already.

Carole's spirits lifted when Colonel Hanson drove through the gates to Quantico. A tall uniformed soldier saluted them and then waved them through. Carole *was* excited for the day with her father, and since she couldn't do anything right away about Max, she figured she might as well try to put the situation out of her mind.

Their first stop was the Officers' Club. Colonel Hanson showed her the ballroom where they held dances on holidays and the lounge where officers could read the newspapers. Everywhere they went, men and women stopped to speak with Colonel Hanson and meet Carole. It was the same during lunch. Carole's father could barely eat his turkey club sandwich because he was so busy introducing her.

"Phew!" he said, as they got back into the jeep after lunch. "I thought we'd never escape! I never realized how much work it is having such a pretty daughter."

"Pretty daughter?" Carole teased. "How about having such an important father—I'm exhausted!"

"Not too exhausted for a trip to the stables, I hope?" Colonel Hanson asked.

"Oh, I think I might be able to stay awake for that," Carole said. Actually, she could hardly wait to pay a visit to the base stables where she had ridden so many times.

The barn and paddocks looked exactly as Carole remembered—only half as big. She fairly leapt out of the jeep and ran inside the barn.

"Soda Pop! You're still here!" she cried, glimpsing the palomino Shetland pony that most of the beginners rode. Carole gave the pony a big hug over the stall door.

"You think we'd ever get rid of him?" a familiar voice asked.

Carole spun around. Margery Tarr stood at the end of the aisle, pitchfork in hand. "Margery!" Carole said. She went to hug her former riding instructor. Margery was the daughter of General Peter Tarr, a close friend of Colonel Hanson's. She had been teaching riding to children on the base since she was fourteen. She was twenty-six now.

"I thought you'd be happy to see each other," Colonel Hanson said.

Margery greeted the Colonel. "Excuse my appearance, sir, but—" she began.

"No need to explain," Colonel Hanson said. "Carole looks just the same most of the time, so I'm used to it."

"But you're beautiful!" Carole protested.

Margery and Colonel Hanson laughed. Only Carole would call someone dressed in muddy boots and breeches with hay all over her "beautiful." But Margery was beautiful. She had dark brown hair and pale skin and twinkling brown eyes. No doubt she had hundreds of boyfriends and was probably even engaged to—

"You're not married, are you?" Carole blurted out.

Margery laughed again. "Not yet, Carole," she said. "I'm still enjoying life as a single gal," she said.

"Do you want to go to a Fourth of July picnic at Pine Hollow?" Carole asked.

Margery looked somewhat taken aback by the sudden change in topic, but she agreed good-naturedly. "Sure, that would be really fun. I always like to visit the stables there."

Colonel Hanson eyed Carole suspiciously. Unlike Margery, he had a pretty good idea what Carole was up to. But he wasn't about to stand in the way of a friendly invitation.

"Then I'll see you on the Fourth," Carole concluded happily.

"Great," Margery said.

"And now that that's settled, I'm afraid Carole and I should really be off. We've got an office to visit, barracks to inspect, and a firing range to view," Colonel Hanson said.

"Sounds fun," Margery said. "And we'll have time to catch up on the Fourth. So enjoy your day on base, Carole." She gave Carole a quick hug good-bye.

Sitting in the jeep, Carole sent a mental thank-you up to Cupid. She was positive that Max and Margery would hit it off.

The next stop was a large brick building where Colonel Hanson had his office. He wanted to introduce Carole to his administrative assistant, Sergeant Major Kiernan. A smiling woman met them at the door. "You must be Carole," she said kindly.

"Carole, meet Sergeant Major Kathleen Kiernan, the highest-ranking noncommissioned officer on base," Carole's father said.

Carole's jaw dropped. The officer was young, pretty, and thin. She wore her black hair pulled back neatly into a bun. Recovering her composure, Carole shook hands with Sergeant Kiernan.

"I've got a couple of things to take care of, so I'll leave you two to get to know each other," Colonel Hanson said.

This time it didn't take Carole any time at all to extend the invitation for the Fourth of July picnic.

"I'd love to go, but I'm planning to spend the day with my daughter," Sergeant Kiernan explained. "I'm a single mom, so I don't get to see her as often as I'd like."

"That's okay," Carole said. "You can bring her, too."

"Really? That would be great. She just loves horses, so it'll be a real treat for her."

"Perfect," Carole said.

"Now let me show you around while your dad's busy," the sergeant offered. Carole prepared herself to be bored. She just wasn't that interested in office work, even on a Marine base. Little did she know that five other single women worked in the adjoining offices. Before her father returned, Carole had convinced all of them to come to the picnic, too. There were even two married women who got so excited by Carole's enthusiasm about the horses and games that they wanted to come, and Carole just didn't have the heart to say no. She couldn't wait to tell Lisa and Stevie. They would be so excited at her success.

When Colonel Hanson came to pick her up again and take her out to see the barracks, she had no more idea of what he did in his office than before, but she had half a dozen wife candidates lined up for Max. Carole decided that maybe she should forget her idea to ride, train, and vet horses professionally when she got older and start a singles dating service instead!

STEVIE MANAGED TO arrive at Pine Hollow the next morning only fifteen minutes late, instead of several hours. She hustled to catch up with Lisa and Carole, who were all set to go on a trail ride.

Catching a glimpse of the two of them leading Barq and Starlight by Topside's stall, she called, "Two seconds and I'll be all tacked up—promise!"

"You know," Stevie continued, leading Topside out of his stall a few minutes later, "it's not true what they say. Money *can* buy happiness."

"Why do you say that? You're not thinking of charging admission to the picnic, are you?" Lisa asked. She was always suspicious of Stevie's money-raising schemes, many of which had been known to backfire.

"No, nothing of the kind. Even though Max is going to make the perfect husband, I don't think we need to make people pay to catch a glimpse of him. I was just thinking how happy I am that I decided to pay Michael to do the dusting and clean the bathrooms so that I could go trail riding with you guys. Now, if only my mother would have the same realization and decide to pay someone to clean the house, everything would be perfect."

"But why should she, when she has you?" Carole teased.

"Exactly. And we're free," Stevie said ruefully. Even though the Lakes were well-off, Mrs. Lake didn't like to pay for things that she felt her children could do for themselves.

Carole and Lisa had tied Starlight and Barq to the rings on the outside of the barn while they waited for Stevie. As all three walked in that direction, they overheard Max instructing someone on how to tack up. "That's weird," Stevie said. "Doesn't he have a lesson in about two minutes?"

Lisa nodded. "Yeah, and usually he'd get another student to help, or ask Red." Red O'Malley was the head stable hand. He could always be counted on to help a beginner, give horsey advice, or just have a talk with.

Coming around the corner, they saw Delilah cross-tied in the aisle. Max had a bridle slung over one shoulder and a saddle in his hands. Deborah Hale looked on attentively. Max was speaking very patiently.

"Now, do you remember how to put the saddle on?" he asked gently.

Deborah stared at Delilah's back. "Umm," she said nervously, "you, um, put it in the middle of the back."

The Saddle Club all felt a pang of pity for Deborah. They knew she was about to receive a harsh lecture from Max. If he told students something once, he expected them to remember it for good.

To their surprise Max bit his lip. "Right—that's right. That is definitely right. *Eventually* the saddle should be just about in the middle. But the important thing to remember is that you put the saddle forward on the withers and then slide it back toward the croup—and not vice versa—so that the hair underneath lies flat. Okay?"

Deborah nodded unhappily. "Okay," she said in a whisper.

Stevie, Lisa, and Carole looked at each other in amazement. Whatever had been getting to Max earlier in the week was obviously still distracting him. Not only was he being patient and encouraging and understanding with a student who had failed to remember his previous instructions, he was also about to be late for a lesson, and, as far as The Saddle Club knew, Max Regnery the Third had never been late for a lesson in his whole life.

"He doesn't have time to put up with this," Stevie said.

"Why don't we offer to help out?" Carole whispered.

"I'll take Topside and wait outside. You guys tack up Delilah since you're a little faster," Lisa said. Carole handed the reins to Lisa, and she led the bay gelding away.

"Hi, Max. Hi, Deborah," Carole said.

The two looked up in surprise. They had been so engrossed in the lesson that they hadn't noticed The Saddle Club standing there watching.

Deborah looked relieved at the interruption. She greeted them warmly.

"Listen, Max, we know you've got that adult class starting right now, so why don't we tack up Delilah for Deborah?" Stevie asked.

Max looked uncertainly from Deborah to the girls and back to Deborah again. Finally he asked, "You really want to tack up Delilah?"

"That's right," Carole said cautiously. Was it her imagination, or did Max look vaguely annoyed at her offer?

"Well, all right," Max said. "But make sure you check over the tack carefully." He nodded good-bye and hurried away to teach the lesson. As he rounded the corner, he sneezed violently. "Ah-ah-ah-CHOO!" reverberated down the aisle.

"Sure, Max," Carole said under her breath. "I'll check

over everything." She was a little insulted that Max would even remind her and Stevie to do something so basic, but she gritted her teeth and told herself that it never hurt to be reminded of important rules of horsemanship.

The look on Stevie's face told Carole that her friend was telling herself the same thing.

The two of them got Delilah tacked up in a jiffy. Deborah thanked them politely. "I'm just not used to horses yet, I guess," she said.

"Don't worry," Carole said. "Max'll have you riding in no time."

"I don't know," Deborah said doubtfully. "It's a lot easier writing articles about them than learning to groom and tack up and ride them."

"Are you kidding?" Stevie said. "That's easy compared to being a big journalist! I mean, look at us, we all know a lot about horses, and we can all ride, and we're not even in high school yet. What you do is really hard. If you think about it—" Stevie stopped midsentence when she saw the crestfallen look on Deborah's face. Somehow what she had been trying to say had come out the wrong way. She had meant to compliment Deborah and seemed to have ended up insulting her instead. Now she didn't know *what* to say.

"Um, have a nice ride," Carole said, trying to come to Stevie's rescue. Deborah mumbled her thanks and led

Delilah slowly toward the indoor ring. Stevie and Carole watched her go.

"Is she still writing articles about the track?" Stevie asked.

"I guess so," Carole said. "Otherwise she probably wouldn't be here. I don't think she likes horses that much."

"Yeah, I guess she really has to do a lot of research for the articles," Stevie said.

"Anyway, it's too nice of a day to worry about people who don't like riding. Come on, we've got a picnic to discuss," Carole said.

The two of them joined Lisa, mounted up, and, by silent mutual consent, headed for Willow Creek, their favorite summer spot, at a brisk trot.

When they entered the woods and slowed to a walk, Lisa brought up the subject they'd all been thinking about. "Isn't it funny how many attractive, single women you can find once you start looking?" she asked.

"It's incredible!" Carole said. She related her successful day at the base with Margery Tarr, Sergeant Kiernan, and the others.

"Good job," Stevie said. "And I've got good news, too. First, I saw one of our old baby-sitters jogging yesterday, so I ran alongside her until she agreed to show up. Secondly, Dad was feeling sorry for us last night, so he took us to TD's, and I finally convinced the waitress to take the day off and come."

"How'd you do that?" Lisa asked.

"I promised not to order another blueberry, hot-fudge, caramel, pistachio sundae with nuts and strawberries ever again."

"You'd do that just for Max?" Carole said, in mock amazement.

"It's a tough sacrifice, but somebody had to do it," Stevie said.

"Gee, with Carole's six and your five and my two—" Lisa began.

"Two?" Carole asked. "I thought there was just the model."

"Oh, I forgot to tell you that I invited my dad's secretary, Nicole Gray. I've only met her once, but I remember she has very long legs, and those can come in handy for riding. It's easier to balance, and you look better on a horse."

"Good point," Stevie said. "I haven't really been considering conformation much at all. I was thinking more in terms of stamina and intelligence."

"Stamina and intelligence alone don't make a winner," Carole pointed out judiciously. "You've got to have the correct build, too."

"But remember, the conformations of the sire and dam

have to suit each other, too, to produce the best off-spring," Lisa said.

"True," Stevie said. "I mean, the son of a Shetland and a Thoroughbred could never be a Derby winner, no matter how nice the Shetland was."

"Exactly," Carole and Lisa said in unison. Then Carole added, "I must say, with Margery Tarr's conformation and intelligence and Max's general good breeding, you could really have something nice."

"Don't forget temperament," Stevie put in. "And after putting up with four Lakes, our old baby-sitter, Holly, has got nerves of steel."

"Same goes for my dad's secretary, Nicole. And I do think a bay—I mean, brunette—would be a nice match for Max," Lisa said.

"Can't argue with that," Carole replied.

When they reached the creek, all three dismounted. "Mm, that water looks cool. I can't wait to wade in it," Stevie said.

"I'll hold the horses first," Carole volunteered. None of The Saddle Club was ever foolish enough to tie a horse by his bridle. It might look cool on TV Westerns, but it was really quite dangerous. If a horse got spooked and tried to bolt, he could panic, get tangled, hurt his teeth, or worse. So if they didn't have halters and lead ropes along, they took turns holding the horses.

61

Carole took all three pairs of reins while Lisa and Stevie stripped off their boots and socks and dangled their feet in the water. Once they were settled, talk of the picnic could continue.

Lisa counted off on her fingers the number of people that were coming. "Let's see—Tiffani the model, Nicole, my dad's secretary, six people from the base, right, Carole?"

"Actually," Carole remembered, "there are eleven people coming from Quantico: six single women, one little girl—Sergeant Kiernan is divorced but has a daughter—and, uh, two married women and their husbands."

"Married?" Stevie asked. "What are you trying to do, get them divorced?"

Carole laughed. She explained how she just hadn't been able to bring herself to tell them not to come.

"That's okay, I'm sure they'll have fun," Lisa said. She did some quick mental arithmetic. "Wow, that means eighteen extra people, including the three Cartwright sisters, the waitress, and Stevie's baby-sitter."

The conversation stopped momentarily as all three girls imagined the hoard of eligible women—plus married couples and child—descending upon Pine Hollow and, more important, upon Max.

"Who do you think will win?" Stevie asked after a minute.

"Stevie," Lisa admonished, "it's not a contest!"

"Not a contest?" Stevie said. "Are you kidding? With Max Regnery the Third up for grabs, and Max the Fourth at stake, I'd say every single woman from Boston to Baton Rouge would want to show up for the trials. He's a pretty great trophy in the husband-hunting game, you know."

"It's true," Carole said, a touch wistfully. "I hope I'll marry someone just like him—in twenty years or so, that is," she added hastily.

"Still planning on having the entire wedding on horseback like Dorothy and Nigel?" Stevie asked playfully. Carole's intention to canter—rather than walk—down the aisle was well-known to The Saddle Club. The girls had recently helped stage a wedding at Pine Hollow between two famous horse people, trainer Dorothy DeSoto and British Olympian Nigel Hawthorne.

"That's right," Carole said. "And we'll wear pink coats and stocks instead of black tie."

"And have a carrot wedding cake so the horses can enjoy it, too," Stevie finished.

"Hey," Lisa chimed in, "that reminds me. We'd better figure out some way to feed all of these extra people on the Fourth. It is a picnic and cookout, after all. And Mrs. Reg will never have enough hot dogs and hamburgers and stuff unless we tell her." It was typical of logical Lisa to think of the practicalities in any Saddle Club scheme.

Her foresight had saved them all from any number of fiascoes.

This time, however, Stevie was a step ahead. "Oh, I thought of that already," she said airily. "It's Chad's turn to cook for us again on Saturday, so I'll just tell him to allow for seventeen extra."

"Okay, so the food problem is solved," Lisa said. She and Stevie had both taken turns holding the horses, and they were now making their way slowly back to Pine Hollow. "Or at least, I'm going to assume it's solved." She turned around in her saddle to give Stevie a meaningful glance.

"Assume away," Stevie said with a slightly wicked grin.

"But there's another question. How are we going to get Max to meet all of these women? With any other guy, you could safely predict he would be interested in meeting tons of eligible women. But for all we know, Max will be too busy with the students and horses to even say hi."

"Then I'll drag him over," Stevie said grimly. "There's

no way I'm going to let him waste this opportunity and put us back to square one."

"Wait a minute, I've got an idea," Carole said. "Lisa, you made me think of it. Maybe he could do some kind of introduction to the horses at Pine Hollow. We'll just say that our friends want to try riding and learning more about horses."

"Do you think he'd do it?" Stevie asked.

"Absolutely. Look how nice and patient he was with Deborah. I was thinking—I'll bet he's like that with all the single women," Carole said.

"You think so?" Lisa asked dubiously.

"Sure," Carole replied. "What else would explain how nice he was being? I've never watched an adult lesson, but I'm sure he's easier on them than on the younger riders."

"Actually, he does get after them, too," Stevie said. She explained that she had once given a jumping demonstration to a beginning adult class, and that Max had been barking commands nonstop.

Carole wrinkled her nose. "But were there any single women in the class?"

"I don't know," Stevie admitted.

"Anyway, even if there were, that was a long time ago —probably before Max felt so lonely," Lisa pointed out, warming to Carole's theory. "Now he knows he needs a wife."

"Exactly," Carole said. "And if he's as nice to the women at the picnic as he is to Deborah, they're all going to think he's wonderful, and he's bound to find at least one of them irresistible."

Stevie nodded, then looked at her friends. "Okay, so who's going to be the one to tell Max that more than a dozen strangers—who also happen to be young, attractive, single, women—are coming to the picnic?"

For the first time that day, silence fell among The Saddle Club.

BACK AT PINE HOLLOW, there was the normal walking, untacking, and grooming to take care of. Max was bustling about as usual, but somehow neither Lisa, Carole, or Stevie found the exact right moment to approach him. Finally they regrouped in the tack room to soap their saddles and bridles. One look at each other, and they all knew no one had mentioned the picnic to Max yet.

"We've invited all these people—we *have* to tell him," Lisa said.

"Yeah, but he's going to think it's so weird! And what we're up to will be so obvious," Stevie moaned.

The tack-room door opened and Mrs. Reg entered. Max's mother was a favorite with The Saddle Club and with everyone else at Pine Hollow. She was as hardworking and knowledgeable as Max and always willing to lend an ear to solve a problem. Unfortunately, this problem wasn't one that she could find out about. *Nobody* was going to point out Max's problem to his mother! Stevie, Lisa, and Carole looked down glumly at their tack.

"Why the long faces, girls?" she asked. They all made an effort to brighten up and smile.

"Maybe I've got some good news that will cheer you up," she said. "I was looking at our books last night, and this past year was one of Pine Hollow's most successful in terms of the number of students taking lessons here. And we've had more new adult riders this summer than any summer before, which is good because adults tend to stick with it once they start. I can't wait to tell Max, he'll be thrilled."

"New adult riders?" Carole repeated. "Do you think maybe it's the start of a trend?"

"Oh, sure," Mrs. Reg said. "You know how it goes. One woman decides to take up riding, and then all her friends get interested, too."

"That's great!" Stevie said.

"It's the perfect solution," Lisa murmured.

"Solution?" Mrs. Reg asked. "I didn't know there was a problem."

"It's a solution to—to adults not getting enough exercise," Lisa concluded lamely.

"Why, look at you three—how you're beaming from ear to ear. I'd say that's the Pine Hollow spirit!" Mrs. Reg declared. She continued through the tack room to her office, closing the door behind her.

Stevie threw her sponge in the air triumphantly. "Maybe our guests won't seem so out of place, after all," she said.

"Even so, I don't think we should really announce the fact that the people we invited to the picnic are almost all young women," Lisa said.

"But at least, after Mrs. Reg's news, it might seem a tiny bit more normal," Carole said. "And anyway—" She stopped short as the door opened once again and Max came in. He was carrying two saddles and two bridles.

"Did someone forget to hang up their tack?" Lisa asked sympathetically. She knew how angry Max got when he found tack lying around the barn.

Max gave her a quizzical look. "No, I just offered to help someone out, as, may I remind you, we're all supposed to do at Pine Hollow." He hung up his own bridle and saddle and then put the other tack on Delilah's rack. Stevie gave the thumbs-up sign behind his back: So far Max hadn't gone back to his disapproving self, at least as far as the single women were concerned.

"Max, could we have a word with you about the picnic?" Carole asked. When Max nodded, she plunged right in, telling him how they'd invited some friends to the picnic and how holding an introductory class might be a good idea. "It might even bring some new riders to Pine Hollow," she finished brightly.

"Great. Sounds like an excellent idea. I'm always happy to show Pine Hollow and the horses to anyone who wants to see them. And in return, I have a favor to ask of you," Max said.

Stevie, Lisa, and Carole stared. Their minds raced, wondering if there was anything Max could say to ruin the now-perfect plan.

"I was thinking we could have a mounted-games demonstration," Max said.

All three of them let out a collective sigh of relief. "I've been trying to get some more students interested in signing up for the Pony Club games," Max continued, "but it's always easier to interest people once they've seen them played—especially by a crack team like you three."

The Saddle Club was so relieved, that the compliment —one of Max's rare ones—hardly sank in. They immediately set about planning what games they would play. A few were definites.

"I always like the costume race," Lisa said. That game involved riding down to the end of the ring, dismounting, dressing up in a costume, getting back on, racing back to the starting line, and undressing so that your teammate could then dress up in the same clothes.

"Me too," Carole agreed. "And you can't leave out the

70

traditional relay race with the batons. It's simple, so everyone can understand it."

"Simple but boring," Stevie said. "Personally, I think the one that has the most crowd appeal is the Super Soaker Target Shoot."

Lisa and Carole had to admit that she was right. Spectators seemed to love to watch riders squirting huge water guns and—most of the time—missing the target and soaking each other, the horses, and even the spectators themselves. In any case, whichever games were chosen, they would be a great diversion for the extra guests—all eighteen of them. Saturday could hardly come fast enough.

"Now THIS is what I call a good, old-fashioned Fourth of July picnic," declared Mrs. Reg. She paused with her case of soda to survey the scene at Pine Hollow. Carole, who was helping her carry drinks from the car to the tables, paused beside her.

Together they looked out over the grounds. A long buffet table covered in a red-checked tablecloth had been set up on the grass. People swarmed around it, helping themselves to pasta salad, cole slaw, and drinks. The waitress from TD's had contributed two gallons of ice cream that was keeping cold in a cooler of ice. There were groups of young students—the picnic was *supposed* to be for them—standing and talking or sprawled on the lawn. In the background horses grazed contentedly, perking an occasional ear to hear what was going on at the picnic. The weather report had called for a "partly cloudy" day, but so far the only clouds in the sky were huge, white, fair-weather clouds.

"It's funny, though," Mrs. Reg observed, heading toward the refreshment table with her case, "I have never, in all my years at Pine Hollow—and that means in all my years period—seen so many attractive young women attend the picnic."

Carole's eyes quickly traveled to where Lisa and Stevie had settled, along with their charges, under a big elm tree.

"I guess it's just what you said, Mrs. Reg," Carole said.

"What did I say?" Mrs. Reg asked.

"You know, about there being a trend and all that for women learning to ride."

Mrs. Reg frowned. "Hmm, so I did. But then—"

"Probably one of them takes lessons, and she brought all of her friends," Carole added hastily.

Mrs. Reg seemed to accept Carole's explanation. "I never can keep track of the adult students. They're always changing their hairdos or going on diets." She glanced back at the group. Everyone was talking and laughing. "Well, at least they're enjoying themselves."

Carole giggled silently. Not as much as we are, she thought to herself. Aloud she said, "I hope they'll all sign up for lessons at Pine Hollow."

"Good girl—always thinking of the stable. Max would approve," Mrs. Reg said.

If he only knew! Carole thought.

"Anyway, I'd better get that grill in the barbecue pit going before we have a mass revolution of the hungry."

After dropping off the sodas with Mrs. Reg, Carole joined Stevie and Lisa under the elm. Unfortunately, her friends were both so busy darting around among the single women that they barely noticed her. Carole was amused to see that Stevie, who had taken Miss Cartwright to the tack room earlier to show her the science project in full bloom, was now stammering her way through an explanation of the different soils.

Carole found the Quantico crowd mingling happily—husbands included. She greeted Margery, Sergeant Kiernan—who introduced her to her daughter, Christine—and the rest. Just as she was about to lie down on the lawn and take a breather, Max showed up.

The Saddle Club leapt to attention. They toured Max around the group, introducing him to everyone, and making sure to treat the women as if they were practically their best friends.

Max shook hands politely. He even smiled a few times, too, but he seemed somewhat mystified by the whole scene. At one point he drew Carole, Lisa, and Stevie aside. "I know all these women are your friends. But aren't they kind of—"

"Friendly?" Stevie broke in. "Yeah, I guess that's what makes them so great, huh, guys?"

"Definitely," Lisa said. "Well, we'd better get in line for a burger or they'll be gone. Max?"

"Uh, you go ahead. I've got some things to take care of in the stable," Max said. "And then I want to make an important announcement."

"Are you sure you can't stick around?" Carole asked. Max, however, was already ten paces away from them.

"Now you've scared him off," Stevie said to Lisa.

"*I* scared him off? More like *they* terrified him. And besides, I did want to get a hamburger," Lisa answered defiantly.

The three of them looked over toward the barbecue, where a small line had already formed. Mrs. Reg and Deborah Hale were doing the cooking.

"I'm surprised she's here," Carole said. "Max isn't going to have much time today to help her with her research."

"That's for sure," Lisa agreed. She giggled. "Did you see his face when we introduced him to Tiffani?"

Stevie grinned, nodding. As the three girls joined the line at the barbecue, Stevie noticed Deborah Hale squinting. Some of the smoke from the fiery grill was wafting into her eyes, and the reporter was wiping away tears.

75

"Let's hope Deborah is better with a hamburger flipper than a saddle," she said. "I'm starved."

When they neared the table, Deborah let out a shriek. "Oh, my gosh! Look at this meat—it's green!" She held up an uncooked, greenish patty for Mrs. Reg to look at. "We've been serving contaminated meat! We've got to find out where it came from right away. People could get seriously ill!"

At Deborah's shriek Stevie ran up to the table, completely horrified. *She* had provided the meat. What if someone had eaten it! She could just see the headline of the *Washington Times*—"Well-known Riding Stable Kills Off Parents, Students: An Eyewitness Account." How could Chad have been so stupid as to purchase rotten beef? Or wait a minute. Maybe he wasn't so stupid after all. In an instant Stevie's fear had turned into fury. She, and everyone else around her, had been duped by none other than Chad Lake and a little green food coloring.

Mrs. Reg glanced at the meat and then looked sharply at Stevie. "Stevie, you wouldn't have anything to do with this, would you, dear?" she asked.

"Absolutely not," Stevie stated. "But brother Chad did—and he's going to pay with his life for this little joke. Don't you see, Mrs. Reg? It's the oldest trick in the book—food coloring."

Carole and Lisa burst out laughing. They knew right away what had happened. Chad had been getting back at

Stevie for wrangling him into doing so much food shopping for the picnic.

Deborah didn't seem to share The Saddle Club's amusement. "You should tell your brother that that's an obnoxious little prank he played. I've covered stories about food poisoning, and let me tell you, it's not a pretty sight," she said heatedly. Her face was bright red from smoke, anger, and embarrassment at being fooled by Chad's joke.

Mrs. Reg put an arm around Deborah to calm her. "Deborah, I know Stevie, and if she says it was only a joke, I'm sure that's what her brother meant it to be. We can be pretty strange at Pine Hollow sometimes. It really takes some getting used to. Isn't that right, Max?" Mrs. Reg asked her son, who had just taken his place in line behind The Saddle Club.

"Isn't what right?" he asked.

"That Pine Hollow can be a confusing place until you get used to it." She tilted her head significantly toward Deborah.

"Oh, right. Definitely," Max said. He didn't seem to know what else to add.

Deborah shrugged and turned back to the grill.

"Listen, this next batch of franks and hamburgers isn't quite ready, so why don't you all sit down and come back in a few minutes?" Mrs. Reg suggested.

Max muttered something about his announcement, then seemed to think better of it.

"What, dear?" Mrs. Reg asked.

"Nothing," he said.

"I've got an idea," Carole said. "This is the perfect time to have the beginner class for all of the new, potential riders."

Max agreed. He told them to bring out Patch for a grooming and saddling demonstration. Stevie ran to the barn while Lisa and Carole rounded up the troops.

In a few minutes Max was standing in a paddock close to the barbecue pit. Surrounding him was a circle of young women who were smiling expectantly.

As with most inexperienced or first-time riders, the women had come in a wide variety of "riding" clothes. Tiffani wore the kind of Western-style outfit you could find at the mall, complete with plaid shirt and cowgirl hat. The Quantico people were mostly neat and workmanlike in their civilian clothes, or "civvies" as Colonel Hanson called them. Holly, Stevie's old baby-sitter, was wearing Lycra jogging pants, aerobics shoes, and a tank top. The Cartwright sisters looked sensible in jeans, hard-soled shoes, and nice T-shirts. Margery Tarr, the only one in breeches, boots, and a button-down shirt, stood watching from a distance. She was interested not in seeing *what* Max taught but *how* he taught, as she often had to teach beginners on base. Carole knew Margery was also hoping to be able to take a ride around the outside course after the picnic.

Once again Max seemed surprised by the ages of the women who had shown up for the introduction. "Boy, I thought they would be closer to your—" he started to whisper to Stevie, who was holding Topside.

"Isn't it great how many young women—I mean, older young women—seem to be taking up riding these days? It's just like your mother said—one gets interested, and then they all do. Our friends are the perfect example. And you know, they have to overcome so much to even get here. A lot of people are prejudiced against adult beginners and treat them differently, as if they shouldn't be there or something."

Stevie paused for breath and saw that Max was looking at her thoughtfully, as if trying to decide if she was telling the truth. Under his breath he said, "It's just that I told people that the guests at the picnic are my closest friends. What will they think?"

Stevie shrugged. Why couldn't Max just tell them—whoever Max meant by "people"—that he was a terrifically popular ladies' man? In order to escape further questioning, she introduced Patch in a loud voice and then said, "And now, the man you've all been waiting for, Max Regnery the Third, manager of Pine Hollow Stables."

Max grew very red, cleared his throat, and without

further ado, picked up a hoof pick and launched into a detailed demonstration on grooming. From the audience Lisa and Carole watched intently to see if he met anyone's eyes in particular or smiled at one woman more than another.

"Can you tell anything?" Lisa whispered.

Carole shook her head.

"Who's he looking at the most?" Lisa asked.

"Patch!" Carole answered.

"Typical!" Lisa whispered back.

All of the women looked very interested in the grooming lesson, and a few asked questions when Max had finished. He answered each one politely and briefly and then started explaining tacking up. Carole and Lisa strained their eyes again but to no avail. Finally Max announced that anyone who liked could form a line and try mounting one at a time. All of the guests hurried into place, the two husbands included.

The first woman in line was Tiffani. Stevie raised her eyebrows at Carole and Lisa as the model bent her left knee, placed her foot in the stirrup and got a helpful boost from Max. Max took his time about making sure her legs hung down correctly and checking her position in the saddle. The Saddle Club exchanged glances: No question Max *had* to notice how long and shapely and perfect for riding her legs were—just like Max the

Fourth's would be! Lisa crossed her fingers. If only Tiffani would be the one! She would be so proud.

They thought the same thing about Sergeant Kiernan's legs, the waitress from TD's legs, and Nicole's. Holly and the Cartwright twins were a close second. Max spent several minutes with each woman, chatting with her in a friendly tone to help her feel more comfortable five feet off the ground. Stevie, Lisa, and Carole were dying of excitement. Max seemed totally interested in talking with each and every woman. The girls were a little disappointed when he seemed just as interested in talking with the two married women and their husbands, as well as six-year-old Christine Kiernan. The girls didn't let it bother them for long though. His behavior, they decided, only helped to show just how great a guy he was.

When Margery got to the head of the line, she smiled and asked, "Do you really think I should risk it?"

Max looked at her sharply. His face relaxed into a wide grin. "Margery Tarr!" he exclaimed, shaking hands with her. "I haven't seen you since we fence judged at that three-day event last fall. What brought you to Pine Hollow?"

"I didn't think you'd remember," Margery said. She explained her connection with Carole, adding that she was hoping to get a ride on Dapper later on, one of Max's experienced hunters. Carole, meanwhile, was practically jumping out of her skin. She was sure Max was going to choose Margery. They would be perfect together. Both loved horses, riding, giving lessons—everything you needed to make a marriage work.

"I can't believe I never put two and two together. I knew Carole had learned to ride at Quantico, and I knew she'd had a great teacher, but I never realized it was you," Max said.

Margery nodded modestly. "I had some good talent to work with," she said.

Carole beamed.

"Hey, do you still have that same boyfriend?" Max asked suddenly. "He's such a great guy."

"I sure do. And he still refuses to learn to ride. I guess I . . ."

Carole didn't hear another word. Her heart sank. So much for being sure. She could have sworn Max would go for Margery and vice versa. And here Margery had had a boyfriend all along! And what was worse, Max knew about him and didn't seem at all upset.

Lisa elbowed her gently and mouthed, "Too bad."

Carole made herself smile. There was no sense feeling bad about Margery when Max had twelve more women to think about, all of whom were probably madly in love with him by now. But she did feel the tiniest bit betrayed that Margery's boyfriend didn't even ride. How could

Margery possibly get along with him? Sometimes adults were impossible to figure out.

"My gosh, what's happening?" Lisa's startled question interrupted Carole's thoughts. Right beyond the paddock fence, where the barbecue pit was, a small burst of flames lit up.

"Oh, no!" they heard Deborah yell. Mrs. Reg had been leaning on the fence watching the lesson, but she immediately picked up a bucket of ice and sloshed it over the grill. Smoke poured off it.

"Nothing to worry about!" she called. "A hamburger just caught fire for a second. Are you okay?" she asked Deborah more quietly.

Deborah nodded. Her eyes were filled with tears.

"Is she all right?" Max echoed. He turned to Stevie, who was closest to him.

"Yeah, it looks like the smoke really got to her though," Stevie said. "You should splash your eyes with cold water!" she yelled to Deborah.

Deborah gave Stevie a stricken look. Then she put down her barbecue tools and fled toward the stable. Max watched her go.

"That was good advice, Stevie," Lisa said. "I know that's what Dad always tells me to do when the kitchen gets smoky."

"Ahem," Carole said. Max turned to her. Carole nodded toward the group who was waiting to be told what to do. Max looked back at the stable.

"Maybe I should see . . ." He let his voice trail off.

"If there are any more questions?" Lisa asked hopefully.

"Uh, yeah," Max said. "Right."

WITHIN HALF AN hour after the introductory lesson had ended, Mrs. Reg and Stevie, who had taken over Deborah's place at the barbecue pit, had the grill going again and were cooking up hamburgers and hot dogs in a jiffy. A few of the parents had brought brownies and cookies, and Colonel Hanson had provided a watermelon, so there was plenty for dessert, too.

Stevie was gleefully holding forth to the people in the hamburger line. They kept asking why the meat was green when it wasn't even St. Patrick's Day. To each new group she announced loudly, "Wondering why the meat's off-color? Call Willow Creek's own Mrs. Lake, a mother guilty of cruel and unusual punishment. She makes her children slave all day doing housework and cooking so that they have to resort to dyeing food for fun and entertainment."

Everyone seemed to be having a great time. Eventually Deborah reappeared and asked for a nongreen burger. She was leaning against the fence by herself, eating quietly and watching the crowd.

"Taking notes, I'll bet," Lisa whispered.

Carole nodded. "For the big story on food poisoning at Pine Hollow," she said.

They giggled to themselves. They had tried talking with Deborah for a while, but it was hard because they didn't think they should bring up horses or riding in case she thought they were bragging or being insensitive. Finally they had given up and had joined the laughing group of Max and his new, adoring fans. The women seemed to be competing with each other to see who could ask Max the most questions about riding and act the most interested in Pine Hollow.

"Who owned Pine Hollow before you, Max?" Holly asked.

"That was my father, Max the Second," Max replied.

"And how about before that? Was it Max the First?" Miss Cartwright asked.

"That's right," Max said. "My grandfather, about whom there are many legends." A murmur went through the crowd.

Stevie, Lisa, and Carole grinned. They knew the story

on Max the First: There *was* no story. He had just been an everyday guy whom people made up wild rumors about.

"And what about after?" the waitress asked. "I suppose that would be Max the Fourth?"

Max smiled enigmatically. "Should I be lucky enough to marry and have an heir, yes, I suppose it would be Max the Fourth."

"Or Maxine!" Stevie, Lisa, and Carole shouted in unison. Everyone laughed, and some of the women clapped.

"Amen to that," Mrs. Reg said.

"Nothing could please me more," he said. Under the watchful eyes of The Saddle Club, he excused himself and went to get some dessert. The girls trailed him, pretending to want more dessert.

"Are you having a good time, Max?" Stevie asked.

"I'm having a marvelous time," Max said. "Your friends are really great fun. It was a good idea to invite them. And now I think I'll sit with my mother for dessert. I want to talk with her for a moment."

"Oh, no!" Carole cried. "I mean, please sit with us. It's the big picnic, and it only comes once a year."

Max looked down at the three pairs of pleading eyes. "All right, if it really means so much to you. I suppose I can speak with Mother later. But I do have an announcement to make," he added firmly.

"An announcement?" Stevie asked. "Oh, I get it." She

waved her hands to silence the crowd. "Everyone, Max has an announcement to make. And that is that the mounted-games demonstration will start in five minutes. So get your seats now!" She turned back to Max. "Good thinking," she said. "We've got to keep this show on the road, or the fireworks will be starting before we know it." Another Pine Hollow tradition was watching the town fireworks from a small hill behind the stable, an excellent spot to see them from.

"Okay," Stevie continued. "Carole, you saddle Nickel and Dime and Penny and Quarter so we can have four teams. Lisa, we need the targets set up. I'll—"

"Actually," Max broke in, "that wasn't the announcement I had in mind. But it's all right. I'll make it later. Come on, Lisa, I'll help you with the targets."

Before you could say "Super Soaker Target Shoot," the picnic had transformed itself into a games practice, with The Saddle Club in charge. First, Lisa, Carole, and Stevie did a mock costume relay race, competing against another team of three. Then they dismounted and turned the ponies over to younger riders, first showing them how to mount and dismount as fast as possible.

There would be two different relay races. Carole explained the objectives to the parents, other students, and single women.

"In the first race, riders will have to take a baton, ride down to the flagged barrel and back, and hand off the baton to the next rider. The bigger kids are going to play a different game, involving a squirt gun and target. Basically, they'll be trying to ride down to the target, hit it with the water, ride back, refill the gun, and hand it off. This one is a Pine Hollow favorite, created by Stevie Lake, who is the world's best at Super Soaker Target Shoot."

The crowd clapped politely at Carole's explanation and waited for the signal that would begin the races. Mrs. Reg poised at the end of the ring to drop the flag. She raised her hands—and one of the Super Soaker targets fell over.

"Time out!" Stevie called at once. She ran down to the end of the ring to examine the target, now lying on the ground. The easel that had been holding it up had fallen over. Stevie saw why. One of the legs had completely snapped from the weight of the target. She thought fast. After such a great introduction, everyone was really interested in the race. And come sign-up time for Pony Club games, it was crucial that Horse Wise have a big, enthusiastic turnout. In other words, the games must go on! The only logical solution was to have somebody hold up the target.

Stevie glanced around. Deborah was still standing alone and looked kind of out of it—as if she didn't know where to go or what to do with herself. Stevie knew that when she was feeling that she didn't fit in somewhere, she liked to have something to do. That always made it easier to fit in.

"Hey, Deborah!" Stevie called enthusiastically. She hurried over to the woman's side. "Are you busy right now?" she asked.

Deborah brightened visibly. "No, not at all. I was just getting ready to watch the games, but I guess you're having trouble, huh?"

Stevie nodded. "That's exactly what I wanted to talk to you about, actually. I was wondering if maybe you could hold up the other target, because the easel that *was* holding it up collapsed and broke. I don't know what else to do—everyone's all set to watch."

Deborah smiled warmly. "I'd love to help out in any way I can," she said.

"Great!" Stevie practically yelled. In no time at all, she had maneuvered Deborah into position and reorganized the riders, who were beginning to get bored waiting.

Carole, Lisa, Stevie, and Betsy Cavanaugh, another experienced Pony Clubber, each had a team of younger riders to calm down, instruct, and root for. Carole and Betsy's teams would be playing the baton game. Lisa and Stevie's teams would play Super Soaker. After each girl had rebriefed her team about the games, Stevie nodded to Mrs. Reg that she could begin the races. The flag dropped, and they were off.

From the very first minute, the audience loved what they saw. Parents and siblings cheered on family members while the experienced games riders took mental notes on whom they should try to recruit. The baton race was fun to watch because the children were so small that jumping on and off Nickel and Dime—even though the ponies were about ten hands high—was no easy feat. Most of the time they half dismounted, half tumbled off.

Meanwhile the Super Soaker was unquestionably, as Stevie had predicted, the biggest crowd-pleaser. Everyone roared when the riders shot the water guns and missed wildly. As usual, they were racing so fast that their marksmanship left a lot to be desired. As long as some of the water hit the target, they were entitled to race back and trade off. At the opposite end of the ring, The Saddle Club stood between the two starting marks, cheering wildly for their teams.

After dusting off a couple of baton-race victims, Betsy Cavanaugh came to join them. "Stevie, I have to hand it to you. You really do make up the best relay races. Or at least the most outrageous," she said.

"The riders are having so much fun—I'm sure more people will want to sign up for the Pony Club games next year," Lisa said.

"The parents and adult students look like they wish they could have a turn," Carole said.

"I must admit, everyone does seem to be having a blast," Stevie said, looking around with a satisfied air.

"Everyone but that poor woman holding up the target, you mean," Betsy said. She pointed to Deborah.

Actually, Deborah *was* having a blast—of water, that is—and she didn't seem to be liking it. Most of the water that missed the target was hitting her.

"Gee, I thought she might enjoy getting splashed. I guess I was wrong," Stevie said worriedly. The frown on Deborah's face told her everything she needed to know.

"I'd love to get soaked on a hot day like this," Lisa said.

"Me, too," Stevie said. "That's why I asked Deborah. I thought it would be fun for her to join in the typical Pine Hollow craziness. I've got to stop the race, though. She's obviously not having any fun."

"You can't stop it now, Stevie," Carole said. "They're on the last time around, with only two more riders to go. Besides, she's soaked already. Five minutes isn't going to matter."

"No, I guess it won't," Stevie admitted reluctantly. She'd have to apologize to the reporter afterward.

She turned back to her team. "Go! Go! Go!" Stevie hollered, watching the last rider on her team refill the water gun and take off toward the target. It was little Christine Kiernan, who had been pressed into service at the last minute, to make a complete team. She galloped down the ring, several lengths in front of her competitor, stopped on a dime, aimed—and got about two drops on the target and the rest on Deborah. Then she spun around and raced back to clinch the victory.

Stevie's team members whooped it up. They all swarmed around her, telling her how much they loved the games and couldn't wait to play more. Mrs. Reg came over and congratulated Stevie and Betsy, whose team had won the baton race.

Stevie thanked Mrs. Reg. "Well, I *should* be able to coach a team to win a game that I invented," she said. The riders laughed.

"I'm glad you gave us that hint about the guns not refilling properly so you have to tilt the bucket," Christine said.

"Shhhhh!" Stevie said. "Never give away trade secrets."

Mrs. Reg shook her head at Stevie. "Tsk, tsk, Stevie Lake," she said.

"The guns don't refill properly?" Lisa asked.

"Well, it's not exactly that—" Stevie began.

"Funny," Lisa broke in. "This one seems to be full." With that, she drenched Stevie with all of the water in the gun.

"Okay! Okay!" Stevie yelled. "I promise I'll never play Super Soaker with those guns again!"

"All right," Lisa said, relenting. "Lucky for you my

team had so much fun, they didn't care who won. Otherwise, I'd have to kill you."

What Lisa said was true. Everywhere they looked, students and parents were discussing the games animatedly and grinning from ear to ear. Only Max seemed less than enthusiastic. He watched the happy scene from a slight distance, his brow furrowed in thought.

"Hey," Stevie said suddenly, remembering her mental note to see about Deborah. "What happened to our target holder? We can compare clothes and see who's wetter."

"There's no contest there," Lisa said. "Deborah's clothes looked like she got caught in a rainstorm. They were absolutely clinging to her. Anyway, she ran into the house as soon as the games ended. She probably wanted to change."

"Maybe she should change her attitude at the same time," Betsy Cavanaugh commented. "She doesn't seem capable of fun."

Although Stevie partially agreed with Betsy, she felt a pang of remorse. First the green hamburgers, and now this. The least she could have done was offer Deborah a towel. She knew from experience that it could be embarrassing to get soaked in front of strangers—Stevie's brothers' favorite summer pastime had been catching her off guard when their friends were over and spraying her with the hose. And even if she wasn't the world's most accommodating guest, Deborah *was* a guest of Pine Hollow, and she deserved the consideration that normally went along with that position.

Oh well, Stevie told herself, there's nothing I can do about her right now, but maybe I can help Max. All day long he had been trying to make his announcement. Stevie, Lisa, and Carole—but mostly Stevie—had cut him off every time so that they could follow their own agenda. Obviously whatever it was meant a lot to him or he wouldn't keep bringing it up. Worrying about the announcement had probably been what kept him from enjoying the games.

Stevie ran into the middle of the crowd, summoning parents, students, and single women from where they'd been sitting. She waved her hands to quiet the conversation. "Everyone, listen up!" she cried. "Max has an important announcement that he's been wanting to make." She glanced around for Max and spotted him standing in the driveway. To her surprise he was staring at a taxi that had just pulled up, a dumbstruck expression on his face.

"Uh, Max?" Stevie called uncertainly.

As she waited for a response, the door to the house slammed. Max turned toward the noise, followed by everyone else. They saw Deborah hurrying toward the cab carrying a big suitcase. She got right in, suitcase first, and didn't look back as it drove away.

"Max?" Stevie asked more quietly.

95

He seemed to notice her for the first time. "Not now," he said. Stevie barely heard him because he spoke in a whisper. Then he ran into the house.

"I have just one question," Lisa said, joining Stevie. "*What* is going on?"

As SOON AS the crowd had resumed chatting among themselves, Lisa and Stevie pulled Carole away from her Quantico friends for a quick conference. No one could come up with a good answer to Lisa's question.

"Maybe there *is* something bad happening at Pine Hollow, and Deborah is going to report it," Stevie said.

"What could possibly be happening here? Max is one of the most reputable horsemen in the business. He'd never do anything dishonest," Lisa said.

"You're right," Stevie acknowledged. "Maybe she left because of the Super Soaker game. I'm sure Max thought it was another careless scheme of mine—getting her to hold up the target—and by leaving, she proved him right."

97

"I think Deborah probably just got sick of being at Pine Hollow—she never seemed that keen on riding—and Max feels bad that he couldn't win her over to it. He's always so disappointed when people don't feel the same way about the place as we do," Carole said.

"Well, then it was pretty rude of her to just take off like that," Stevie said. "She may be upset with me, but why take it out on Max? She could've at least thanked him for trying."

"She probably would have but didn't have time. I'll bet there's a fast-breaking story that she has to cover," Lisa said.

Even though no conclusion seemed perfect, one thing was clear: Max was upset, and the girls wanted to help him as much as possible.

"I propose that we leave the women to their own devices for a while and get busy keeping the picnic running smoothly," Carole suggested.

"Agreed," Stevie said. "What's left?"

"There's the jumping demonstration by the short-stirrup kids, and after that the fireworks," Carole said.

The short-stirrup riders were younger boys and girls who were in their first year of competition. They were eligible to enter the short-stirrup division at horse shows, and the fences they jumped were no higher than eighteen inches. Most of them rode small ponies like Nickel and Dime.

"Okay," Stevie said, "so basically the fences need to be set up in the indoor ring. I'm sure they'll want to regroom the ponies themselves—I saw May fussing over Nickel for hours this morning."

"Don't forget regular evening feeding, haying, and watering," Carole said, ever mindful of the horses.

"Not to mention the stalls, which I'm sure no one has had time to muck out," Lisa added.

Stevie groaned. "All right, then, let's get to it. We'll skip watching the jumping and work inside instead," she said.

As usual, part of Stevie's skill in organization was her ability to delegate most of the work to others. Before long moms and dads and older riders were dragging poles and standards to set up crossbars and tiny verticals in the indoor ring, dragging the hose from stall to stall to refill water buckets, and tossing hay bales down from the loft. The Saddle Club decided they'd do the mucking out.

Red O'Malley's face lit up when he saw them coming with the big cart to haul used bedding to the manure pile. "Are you girls a sight for sore eyes," he said. "My two other hands are off today, and I was wondering how we were going to finish all the stalls before dark. I thought maybe I'd have to ask some of those women who've been hanging around all day for some help."

"Oh, Red, you *wouldn't*," Lisa protested. "They'd get completely filthy."

"You all are filthy half the time," Red pointed out.

"Yeah, but we're different," Stevie said.

"How?" Red asked, teasing them.

"Because we're not twenty-five," Carole said, kidding him right back.

"Yeah, so it's okay for us," Lisa said.

After telling them that they'd still be mucking out stalls when they were *forty*-five, Red thanked them and headed back out to the paddocks to start bringing the horses in for feeding.

"So how should we do this—three on one or three on three?" Stevie asked. She was referring to the number of girls per stall.

"As if you had to ask," Lisa said.

They opened the nearest empty stall and began mucking, taking turns dumping the cart behind the barn. When they had finished four and started on the fifth and last stall on the aisle, Max passed by on the way to his office next door. He barely nodded in their direction.

"Gosh, I hope the jumping went okay—Max still looks kind of disturbed," Carole said.

"He doesn't look like a man who has thirteen women —intelligent, attractive, successful, or all of the above— waiting for him to return," Stevie said.

"Do you think he liked *any* of them?" Lisa asked.

"Oh, *yes*," Stevie replied. "I saw him talking with the Cartwright twins during the games demonstration. He looked so absorbed he hardly even paid attention to the games."

"Really?" Carole said. "Because he and Holly looked like they were hitting it off *quite* well before."

"Max and Holly would look good together. They're the perfect height for each other," Stevie said thoughtfully.

"Yeah, but if we're talking looks, you've got to hand it to Tiffani," Lisa said. There was a pause as they sighed in unison. By powers unknown to Stevie, Lisa, and Carole, Tiffani had somehow managed to remain a vision of model-perfect loveliness all day, in spite of the heat, dust, and horseflesh.

During the pause in conversation, the door to Max's office squeaked on its hinges. Without really trying, they could hear Max and Mrs. Reg talking in urgent, hushed tones.

"Why be stubborn at a time like this?" Mrs. Reg demanded.

"It's *not* stubbornness, Mother. I just know there's nothing I can do," Max answered.

"Nothing? That's not true. You could go after her," Mrs. Reg said.

"Go after her now?"

"That's what your father had to do to get me back."

"Forget it. It's no use. She's never going to speak to me again."

"*She?*" Carole mouthed.

Stevie shrugged and put her finger to her lips.

Mrs. Reg said something inaudible. Max answered more loudly. "It's off. Everything concerning Deborah Hale is off. I'm just thankful I was spared the embarrassment of asking her to marry me in public and then having her run off."

The door closed again, and they heard footsteps retreating. They ran to the stall door and looked out into the aisle. Mrs. Reg was walking briskly toward the house wringing her hands.

Stevie watched her go, afraid to move or speak or even breathe. The Saddle Club had ruined the lives of two people. Not only that, they had ruined any chance of producing an heir for Pine Hollow. She glanced at her friends.

"I have a pit in my stomach the size of a black hole," she announced.

"How could we have been *so* stupid?" Carole asked. "The whole time we thought Max was sick or going crazy because he kept sneezing and forgetting our names, he was falling in love! He must have just been incredibly nervous around Deborah. What were we thinking?"

Lisa just shook her head wordlessly. What they had failed to notice for an entire week was now as glaring as a Fourth of July firecracker: Max needed thirteen single women like he needed thirteen sick horses. He had *al-*

ready found a mother for Max the Fourth—none other than Deborah Hale. Now something had gone dreadfully wrong.

One by one Stevie, Lisa, and Carole started to tick off the problems *they* had created.

"We brought thirteen single women to the picnic where Max was planning to propose marriage to another woman," Stevie said, getting right to the heart of the matter.

Carole winced. "Not only that, but he'd told her that the people at the picnic were his best friends."

"So we made him look like a playboy," Lisa said.

"Which is the furthest thing from the truth," Carole said.

"And we made her cook green hamburgers," Stevie said.

"And we let her get soaked by squirt guns," Lisa said.

"And we didn't get her a towel," Carole said.

"Forget 'we' on those last three," Stevie said. "I'll take the blame."

"She probably thought Max's 'closest friends' hated her," Carole said.

"So why stick around—" Lisa began.

"For more abuse," Stevie finished.

"It was one hundred percent our fault," Carole said.

"And one little announcement from Max would have made everything fine," Lisa said.

"But we wouldn't let him make it," Stevie said.

"So it was two hundred percent our fault," Carole said.

"We *really* messed up," Lisa agreed.

"This could be our biggest mess-up ever," Carole said. "The future of Pine Hollow is at stake, not to mention Max and Deborah's happiness."

"Right. So are we going to sit here, or are we going to stick our noses right back in and *un*-mess-up everything —or is that 'mess-down'?" Stevie demanded.

"Whatever it is, we'd better get cracking, because Deborah is in a taxi headed for we-have-no-idea-where," Lisa said.

"Lisa, I'll take that as a go-ahead from you. Carole?"

"I'm in. If we don't get Deborah back for Max, he might never forgive us. And he's one friend I'm not willing to lose," Carole added sadly.

IN A MATTER of minutes The Saddle Club had put away all the tools, dumped the manure cart, and reassembled in front of the stall. The first thing to be done was to establish a plan of pursuit.

"What'll we say to her when we catch her?" Carole asked. Her friends knew that she was often better at knowing what to say to Starlight than to a person in a tricky situation.

"I haven't quite worked out that part of the plan yet," Stevie said.

"We'll decide what to say when we find her," Lisa said.

"Good," Stevie said. "One, find Deborah. Two, think up something to say. Now, how on earth do we find out where that taxi went?"

"It was orange and white. That means it's a Town taxi. Why don't we just call the dispatcher's office and ask?" Lisa suggested logically.

"Brilliant!" Stevie cried. "To the telephone!"

They sprinted to Mrs. Reg's office. The phone there was allowed to be used only in an emergency—and no one bothered to ask if this counted as one. Carole found the number right away. Practically grabbing the phone book out of her hands, Stevie dialed. "Come on, brainstorm, don't fail me now," she muttered. She put the call on speaker phone so Carole and Lisa could hear the conversation and give advice if necessary.

"Oh, ah, hello," Stevie began when someone picked up. "This is Deborah Hale calling. It's so silly of me, but I've taken about a dozen taxis this week—busy journalist, you know—and, well, I took one from Pine Hollow today, and I seem to have lost a pair of gloves, and I just can't for the life of me remember where I got out, but I'm almost positive I left the gloves there, so I was wondering —do you have a record of where the cab stopped?"

The woman on the other end of the line was clearly not impressed by Stevie's performance—or fooled by her impersonation of an older woman. "Gloves in July? Yeah, right, tell me another," she said in a bored tone.

Stevie shot Lisa and Carole a desperate glance. "Try telling her the truth!" Carole whispered.

"All right," Stevie said in a rush. "I'll tell you what

really happened. We—my friends and I—have ruined someone's life, actually two someones' lives. They were in love, and we got in the way, and now she's run away and left him, and it's all our fault, only she thinks it's his fault, and unless we find her and get her back, we'll have to live with this for the rest of our lives!"

The dispatcher started to laugh. At first she chuckled, but soon she was howling. "Sounds like something in the movies. A modern-day love story, huh? That's the best yet!" she said.

"It's true!" Stevie wailed.

"Yeah, and Romeo's standing next to me—right! But since it's such a good one, I'm gonna do you a favor— give you some credit for imagination. Let's see . . . Pine Hollow pickup. Oh, yeah, here it is. That cab went to the Willow Creek bus stop over on Main. Hey, if you hurry, maybe you can catch Juliet!" The woman broke up into laughter at her own joke.

Stevie didn't mind being made fun of at all now that she had gotten the information she wanted. Before the dispatcher had finished whooping, she hung up to ask what the fastest route to the bus stop was.

"I think you go straight downtown past the mall," Lisa said. "But who are we going to ask to drive us? We can't exactly explain things to Mrs. Reg or Max. And all of the parents are busy with their children, getting ready for the fireworks."

"Actually," Carole said, a gleam coming into her eye, "straight downtown is not *the* fastest route. It's only the fastest route by car, if you get my drift."

"I get it, and I like it, and we're doing it because there's not a second to lose," Stevie said, charging out the door into the tack room. She grabbed bridles and hard hats and tossed them to Lisa and Carole, then took one each for herself.

"What about—?" Lisa began.

"Forget saddles! No time!" Stevie yelled.

The three of them hurried to get Starlight, Barq, and Topside. The horses looked up from their hay and were surprised to have bits placed in their mouths immediately. It was dinnertime, not riding time!

Stevie had mastered the tricky skill of springing up onto Topside bareback, without the help of stirrups. She was mounted in two seconds. Carole gave Lisa ten fingers and tossed her up, then jogged Starlight to the mounting block and swung on herself.

"Ready?" Stevie called.

"Ready!" Lisa and Carole responded in a confident yell. "Remember we have to go as fast as we can, but we can't do anything stupid!" Carole added.

"Right!" Stevie said. "Anything else? Then we're off!"

The horses, knowing something exciting was up, had been prancing around and were eager to go. The girls set out toward the fields at a brisk trot, but soon broke into a canter, an easier gait to sit to.

Lisa was surprised at how easily she could stay on. Stevie and Carole occasionally forgot that she was an inexperienced rider compared to them. Most of the time she didn't mind their forgetting this fact, knowing it was a compliment about how fast she had learned. Sometimes, though, she still worried about being able to keep up with them. Stevie's idea to forget the saddles and save time had surprised her. She had ridden bareback many times before but not usually so fast. Barq's canter was smooth and steady, however, and she soon found herself relaxing her death grip on his mane and getting more involved in the purpose of the ride. "Do you think we'll make it?" she called to Stevie, who was up front, setting the pace.

"We have to!" Stevie yelled.

"There are only about three buses a day out of Willow Creek," Carole pointed out.

"But how do we know we won't miss hers by a minute?" Lisa asked.

"We don't!" Stevie said. With that, all three unconsciously leaned farther forward over their horses' necks, urging them on. In minutes they had crossed two fields, jumping the low brushes and panels in the fences put there to enable the hunt to pass. At such a fast pace, a three-foot fence didn't feel much different from another, bigger stride.

All of a sudden Stevie stopped short and waved to Carole and Lisa to follow suit.

"Oh, no!" Lisa wailed when she saw the white post-and-rail beyond the next crest. The fence marked the beginning of the Biddle property. Notorious in Willow Creek, the Biddles had forbidden all trespassing on their property and threatened to sue anyone who set foot on their land. Normally, riders cut back to the woods to avoid the wrath of Mr. Biddle.

"If we go back now, we'll end up going twice as far," Carole said.

"I'm prepared to risk it," Lisa decided. "There's a chance no one's around to see us."

"Yeah, and there's a chance good ole Biddle will be in the middle of target practice with his hunting rifle and will get off a few quick rounds at some live prey," Stevie said.

"Boy, this is probably the way the Native Americans felt when the European settlers fenced in the land," Lisa said in disgust.

"What a perfect idea!" Stevie practically shouted.

"What idea?" Lisa asked.

"We'll make like Indians and lie flat on the horses to evade discovery. At worst, Biddle will think a few loose horses ended up in his field. Come on!" Stevie set off once more for the property ahead.

When they reached the fence, she carefully unlocked the gate, waved Lisa and Carole through, and closed it behind them. Luckily Topside remembered his trail-horse manners and cooperated perfectly. Then they all lay down as low as they could and trotted stealthily across the field.

At the far end Carole volunteered to do the gate. Opening it was easy enough, but when she tried to hook the latch afterward, Starlight decided to spook at his shadow, nearly unseating Carole, who had been leaning out to finish the job. The gate banged opened with a clash. No cattle were anywhere in sight, so there was no danger of their escaping. But up at the Biddle farmhouse, a dog began to bark furiously.

"Please, Starlight!" Carole pleaded. Unfortunately, Starlight was having too much fun prancing and being a pain and was too excited from the gallop to settle down. Lisa rushed to help. She got the gate right away but not quick enough.

"Hey, there!" Mr. Biddle's voice boomed across the field. "You all stay right where you are. I want to talk to you!"

After a split-second pause, Barq, Topside, and Starlight sprang into a gallop like racehorses coming out of the starting gate. "We'll talk to you later, Biddle!" Stevie screamed into the wind.

Before long the girls could hear traffic once more and knew they were nearing civilization.

"Let's cut through the fairgrounds so that we come out on the right side of the street," Carole yelled. She turned Starlight toward the public park on the outskirts of town. After they rounded a corner, the bandstand came into view almost at once, along with several huge tractor-trailer truck beds. The girls slowed to a trot once they realized what was going on. They had come to the site of the evening's fireworks. Crews of men and women stood around setting up the display. They turned to wave as the girls passed. "Hi-ho Silver!" one called.

"What's the big finale going to say?" Stevie asked good-naturedly.

" 'America the Beautiful,' what else?" one of the workmen answered.

The Saddle Club gave them the thumbs-up sign and hurried along, knowing the bus stop was only minutes away. They ducked through a line of trees bordering the park and emerged on the grassy strip of land that stretched along Main Street.

"Look!" Carole cried. Up ahead passengers were boarding a bus that had just pulled in to the stop.

"Come on!" Stevie urged. They raced toward the stop.

Unbelievably, in front of their eyes, the doors of the bus closed, and it pulled away.

"Stop!" Lisa cried. "Oh, stop!"

Thirty seconds too late, they reached the now-empty stop and pulled up short. Or, at least, Lisa and Carole pulled up. Undaunted—and very foolishly—Stevie crouched lower on Topside's neck, drawing her knees up like a jockey, and raced alongside the bus, waving her arms to try to get the driver's attention. The passengers stared out the window excitedly. When the bus stopped at the first light a few hundred yards away, Stevie pulled Topside down to a walk. She rapped on the door.

The driver opened it slowly, staring at Stevie suspiciously. "Yes?" he asked uncertainly.

"I have to see a passenger on this bus, a Miss Deborah Hale," she announced.

The driver remained impassive.

"Please! It's a matter of love!" Stevie begged.

Shaking his head incredulously, the driver agreed to pull over when the light changed. Stevie watched him park on the grassy verge and trotted behind. He stood up and made an announcement. Then he opened the door again.

"Nobody on board by that name, miss," he said.

"Nobody?"

"What part of the word didn't you understand? 'No' or 'body'?" the driver asked.

"Thanks a lot," Stevie said sarcastically. She was in no mood for humor now that Deborah Hale had somehow slipped through their fingers.

Discouraged, she turned Topside back toward the stop. One of the passengers opened her window and leaned out. "Good luck finding your friend," the smiling woman said. "Anybody who'll chase a bus on horseback deserves to succeed."

A couple of other passengers followed suit. "Hear, hear!" a gray-haired woman called.

"Go for it, cowgirl!" a young boy said.

Stevie managed to smile wanly at them. She thought her attempt at stopping the bus had been pretty dramatic, too, but it was looking more and more as if she might have lost Deborah for good, no matter what heroics she could think up. The thought made her want to get down off Topside and give up. What else could she do?

They had failed. They had ruined Max's life. Not only that—they had triple-handedly caused the termination of one of the great horsey bloodlines of the country.

STEVIE LET THE reins go slack. She idly nudged Topside back in the direction of the bus stop where the others would be waiting. Acting as dejected as Stevie felt, the horse shuffled along with his neck stretched out.

"Good try, boy," Stevie said. She gave him a consoling pat on the shoulder. "It wasn't your fault, Topside. You tried your best. I wish Max could have seen the way we raced after that bus. . . ." She let her voice trail off despondently. Her thighs and seat ached, and her mouth felt as dry as a desert. And it had all been for nothing.

Topside could sense Stevie's disappointment. He barely lifted his head when Lisa and Carole came running up leading Barq and Starlight. They had huge grins on their faces, and Stevie knew why. How was she going to break it to them that Deborah had vanished, after all —that the whole chase had been pointless? Worse than pointless, in fact, since Max would almost definitely get an irate phone call from Mr. Biddle.

"Stevie!" Lisa shouted as she came up. She and Carole turned and fell in beside Topside.

Stevie looked sadly at their two eager faces. Looking down at her hands, she began to explain. "I know, I know. Good try, huh? But that's all it was—Deborah wasn't even on the bus. For all I know, she's halfway to Kalamazoo by now, hating us and despising Max because of us. And after all that. Poor Topside's spent. I guess there's nothing left to do but hack home."

Stevie paused in her speech to sigh. She looked up at her friends to see how they were taking it. To her surprise Lisa and Carole hadn't stopped grinning. "What—?" Stevie began.

"Stevie, *look*," Carole said. She pointed eagerly toward the stop. Stevie raised her right hand to shield her eyes from the strong setting sun. All at once she drew a sharp breath. There, with her suitcase beside her, stood Deborah Hale.

Stevie stared incredulously. "I must be seeing things. It's like those desert travelers who think they see an oasis, but it's really only a mirage. That woman looks suspiciously like Deborah Hale, but of course it's not her."

"She's real, all right," Carole said.

"Then what—?" Stevie pointed in the direction the bus had gone.

"That was a different bus! Deborah's bus doesn't come for another hour," Lisa said. She explained that while Stevie had gone on her mad chase, they had decided to get sodas at the drugstore to cool off. Carole had gone to buy them and had found Deborah inside, buying a Willow Creek newspaper so she could read up on some local news.

"Local news at a time like this?" Stevie asked. She had expected that, if they did find Deborah, she would undoubtedly be completely distraught and crying her eyes out.

Lisa shrugged. "I guess her career really matters a lot to her," she said.

"I'll say," Stevie agreed. She followed Lisa and Carole up to the stop, eyeing Deborah cautiously. "So has anyone made our apologies yet?" she asked.

"Not exactly," Carole said. "When I saw her in the drugstore, I was so shocked, I didn't know what to do. I said hello and asked where she was going, but I didn't get around to telling her that she *can't* go anywhere—I mean, not anymore! Then she left and came out here, and we decided to get you before you galloped off into the sunset again."

"Don't worry—Topside and I have had our fill of wild-goose chases tonight," Stevie said. She took another glance at Deborah. Deborah looked as if she was trying very hard to concentrate on her newspaper but failing. Every so often she looked in their direction curiously.

"I think it's time for a little explanation," Stevie said.

"Me too—before Deborah gets more upset—" Carole said.

"—and confused and annoyed and decides to disappear again," Lisa finished.

Slowly they approached Deborah. She looked up expectantly.

Carole decided to dive right in. "Deborah, we all owe you an apology. A huge apology. You see, we got to thinking about Max—and how old he was—not that he's *really* old or anything—and we thought that he might be kind of lonely, and we'd hate for him to be unhappy, so we decided to—what I mean is—we wanted to make the Fourth of July picnic a sort of a—well, a meeting of eligible—" Carole stopped. Perspiration dotted her forehead, and she was completely flustered. Deborah had raised one eyebrow and now looked puzzled and stern and the tiniest bit amused all at the same time.

Stevie rushed to help Carole. "Here's what happened. First all those single women, then the green hamburgers, then target practice, then the announcement—or the lack of announcement, I guess—then the conversation we overheard, then the race to get here and find you, so,

118

to make a long story short, we're sorry." She looked hopefully at Deborah, who was by now looking utterly confused but trying to suppress a smile.

Lisa sighed. It was up to her to clear the air once and for all. She chose her words carefully. "Deborah, none of us is proud of what we've done this week—even though we did it without knowing what we did. We turned your stay at Pine Hollow into a nightmare. We thought we were helping Max by inviting a lot of women we know for him to meet, and you by trying to include you in Pine Hollow's craziness. We didn't realize that we were just getting in the way. But now that we know that Max was *already* in love, we want to do everything we can to make things right again."

When Lisa had begun speaking, Deborah was smiling politely, nodding as Lisa explained. Then she seemed to do a double take. She grabbed Lisa by the arm. "What did you say? Max was already in love? How could he? I mean, with whom?"

It took about a second for The Saddle Club to absorb that Deborah still didn't know what they meant. "With *you!*" they cried in unison.

"He's been in love with you since he met you!" Carole proclaimed.

Deborah shook her head. "I can't believe it," she barely whispered.

"It's true!" Lisa cried. "He kept saying all day that he

wanted to make a 'very important announcement,' but he never got to it because we kept interrupting. And then we heard him say to Mrs. Reg that he had wanted to ask you to marry him!"

Deborah stared at Lisa. Or, rather, she looked at Lisa, but her eyes stared right through her to some place the girls couldn't see. Then she dropped her eyes down. A few tears fell onto her cheeks, and she wiped them away.

"Don't cry, Deborah," Lisa begged. "There's still time to fix things. I'm *sure* of it." She put an arm lightly around Deborah's shoulders to comfort her. Carole bit her lip. Stevie gulped.

Deborah looked up. She was smiling and crying at the same time. "I'm deliriously happy. I can hardly believe it. Marrying Max would be a dream come true."

Stevie whooped while Lisa and Carole let out huge sighs of relief. So far, none of them had ever cried for joy, but they had heard it was something adults did occasionally.

"Now, if he'll only get around to asking me!" Deborah added.

"What do you mean, asking you? This is the nineties!" Stevie said.

Carole and Lisa shook their heads frantically. The last thing they needed was another Stevie-Lake-never-fail special now that they had un-messed-up almost everything they had messed up to begin with. Stevie, however, was rolling along at full force already.

"When you want to get the scoop on a big story, do you wait for it to come to you?" she asked Deborah.

"Of course not," Deborah replied promptly. "If I didn't go after it, I'd never get the story—or I'd get it so late it would hardly be worth it."

"Precisely," Stevie said.

"So what exactly are you getting at?" Deborah asked, although from the glint in her eye, she already had a hunch about what Stevie was thinking.

"I've got an idea, see," Stevie began.

By the time The Saddle Club reached Pine Hollow, it was fully dark. On their way back through—and this time *around* the fields—they had glimpsed the moon rising and the first stars coming out. It was a clear summer night.

"Perfect night for fireworks," Stevie observed as they crossed the last field and came out onto Pine Hollow's outside course.

"Sure is," Deborah answered with a chuckle. She was riding double with Carole on Starlight.

Carole smiled. During the long walk back, she had had more time to talk with Deborah. Carole realized now that Deborah *was* eager to learn more about horses. But the reporter had been nervous and uncomfortable around the other riders. Knowing how much horses meant to Max had only aggravated the situation. And today at the picnic, she had decided to stay out of the way as much as possible to protect herself. But it was obvious from the questions she asked Carole that she genuinely liked horses. She had even been hesitant about riding with Carole because she thought it might strain Starlight's back. Carole explained that riding double was all right as long as you didn't make a habit of it and made sure that you both sat well forward, not back on the loins.

For her part, Deborah seemed impressed with Carole's knowledge and—even more—with her ability to teach what she knew. All the way home Deborah peppered her with questions. "What's the point of trotting over cavalletti?" "How do you know when to use a crop?" "What's a martingale?" "How do you tell what diagonal you're on?"

After answering all of them, Carole laughed. "Now I understand how you get the big stories. This feels like a Know-Down!" she said. Deborah, of course, asked what a Know-Down was, and so they told her all about Pony Club, Horse Wise, rallies, ratings, and finally, games.

"Oh, so you mean that miserable event where I got completely soaked was supposed to foster horsemanship and friendship, huh?" Deborah inquired.

"That's right," Carole said sheepishly.

"That was completely my fault, Deborah. I forgot to

warn you about the side effects of being a human target," Stevie said.

"That's okay," Deborah said. "If I'd known, I would've carried a water gun myself and shot back."

"You learn fast," Lisa complimented her. Lisa had also gotten a chance to talk with Deborah during the ride. She had asked all about what it was like to be a journalist for one of the country's largest, most respected newspapers.

"It's great," Deborah told her. "There's really never a dull day. You learn so much, and you're constantly on the go. And, you know, you meet the most *interesting* people." She winked at Lisa, who grinned back.

"So I guess in a way, we should all be thankful to the drug ring at the track or you'd never have had to learn about horses, and you'd never have come to Pine Hollow," Stevie pointed out.

"I always say, give credit where credit is due," Deborah said. "Especially when it applies to love or my own byline."

Stevie wanted to clap Deborah on the back. Anybody who could quip the way she could was A-okay in her book. Instead she said, "I have just one more question." They had reached the stable and were about to dismount. "Were you *really* buying the paper to brush up on local news?"

"I most certainly was," Deborah replied indignantly.

Then, trying to stifle a grin, she added, "I was trying to find out if they'd have any use for a reporter from the *Washington Times*—I figured at least then I'd be in the area!"

"You mean you were planning to come back, after all this?" Lisa asked.

"We redheads don't scare off *that* easily," Deborah said, with a toss of her shining hair. She swung down off Starlight gracefully.

"Ah-ah-ah-CHOO!" At the unmistakable sound of Max's sneeze, Deborah and The Saddle Club whirled around.

"Deborah!" Max cried. He ran up to her and, oblivious to Carole, Lisa, and Stevie, embraced her. "Where did you go? I—I thought you had left for good. I—"

Max paused midsentence as he noticed the girls. "How did you get her back?" he asked, all at once putting two and two together. "What's going on? How did they find you?"

Deborah disentangled herself from Max's arms and put a finger to her lips. "You'll learn everything you need to know, all in good time," she told him.

Max was about to protest when, in the near distance, a crowd cheered, drowning out his words.

"The fireworks must have begun!" Stevie yelled.

"If we hurry, we won't miss much," Lisa urged.

Max glared at them, but Deborah took him by the

125

hand. She led him off toward the hill where everyone had gone for the best viewing.

In a flash Lisa and Stevie had their horses back in their stalls. Having walked all the way home, they had cooled off completely from the long gallop. Carole decided to bring Starlight with her. She took every opportunity to expose him to new things and wanted to see how he would behave with the noise and the crowd.

"You know you really should rub down Barq and Topside with liniment," she pointed out reluctantly, joining Stevie and Lisa at the door.

"Carole!" Stevie wailed. "We can't miss the fireworks!"

"Who's going to miss the fireworks?" Red O'Malley demanded, emerging from the feed room.

Lisa sped through an explanation. "You don't say," Red answered. Three heads nodded vigorously.

"Go on, then. I'll do the horses. Never was much of a fireworks fan, anyway."

The Saddle Club looked at one another for a second.

"Well, get going or they'll be over!" Red barked. Stevie and Lisa thanked him profusely—and ran. Carole followed, leading Starlight at a quick trot.

It took only a few minutes to race up the little hill that overlooked the field where the fireworks were being set off. From a distance they could see all of the picnic-goers settled on the blankets that Mrs. Reg always provided.

"We made it!" Stevie hollered, as all three of them joined the crowd. She gave Carole ten fingers to hop up on Starlight for a better view.

"All you missed were the dumb ones at the beginning," little Christine Kiernan told them.

"The end is always the best part, isn't it?" Lisa said to no one in particular.

Willow Creek was known for its fireworks, and this Fourth of July display was no different. Once it really got going, everything was spectacular, both the groundworks —lights displayed from the ground—and the regular fireworks high up in the dark sky. There were dozens of starbursts in different colors up above and then a Catherine wheel from below. Back in the sky there was an astonishing burst of red, white, and blue lights in the shape of the American flag. The crowd cheered happily, including Max and Deborah. They were standing together, slightly apart from everyone else.

Then there was a moment's pause as the technicians reloaded, followed by an unusual-looking set of groundworks.

"It looks like letters, doesn't it?" Mrs. Reg said.

"Probably 'America the Beautiful,'" Holly suggested.

"I don't think so—that's an M," Nicole said.

The crowd fell silent, trying to puzzle out the message. They saw "M-A-R—"

"'Mar'—what's that?" Tiffani asked.

"Wait, it's 'marry'!" Mrs. Reg fairly shouted. Everyone waited breathlessly. "M-A-R-R-Y M—" sparkled across the sky.

"What *is* this?" Margery Tarr asked.

Finally the whole thing appeared: M-A-R-R-Y M-E M-A-X! The crowd seemed to turn as one to look at Max. Max, however, did not have to turn very far. He had eyes for one person only, and she was standing right next to him: Deborah Hale. She gazed up at him steadily.

Max grasped her shoulders. The crowd drew in its breath. Max looked completely overwhelmed by this romantic—not to mention very original—method of popping the question. He tried to speak but instead sneezed violently. Deborah blushed as crimson as her hair. And then, while everyone looked on delightedly, Max Regnery the Third leaned down and kissed Deborah Hale on the lips, sealing the deal.

The kiss got a bigger cheer than any of the fireworks. Stevie, Lisa, and Carole whooped with everyone else. Then they turned to each other and exchanged high fives.

"Best Fourth of July picnic I've ever been to," the TD's waitress said, shaking her head in amazement.

"Then you had a good time?" Stevie asked eagerly.

"Oh, sure," the waitress said. "But you should have told me what this Max guy was into—if I'd known, I would've brought firecrackers instead of ice cream!"

After the younger children had all gone home, taking their parents with them, and Mrs. Reg had disappeared into the house to call relatives with the news, and Red had finally driven off in his pickup, and Deborah and Max had left for Washington to tell her parents, and every last barn chore was finished, Lisa, Stevie, and Carole found themselves alone in the tack room. None of them was eager to part company. As Lisa put it, "What's a Saddle Club success story without a sleepover afterward?"

Fortunately Stevie predicted that her mother would be in a good mood after all the work she and her brothers had put in this week. She was right. Mrs. Lake picked them up, drove them home, and cooked a huge spaghetti dinner, complete with garlic bread, even though the other Lakes had eaten already.

About halfway through the meal, the phone rang. Stevie ran to pick up the receiver. To her delight it was Amy calling for Chad. This was the opportunity for revenge that she'd been waiting for.

Stevie yelled upstairs for him.

"I'll take it up here!" Chad called back.

"Okay!" Stevie called. She held the receiver in her hand, getting ready to make a crack about being "green" with envy that the phone call was for him. But when Chad picked up the upstairs receiver, he sneezed loudly three times in a row. Carole, Lisa, and Mrs. Lake all looked up at the noise. Quietly Stevie hung up the phone.

Turning back to the table, she commented, "Looks like hay fever is starting all over again."

"Do you think Chad's getting sick?" Mrs. Lake asked.

"Don't worry, Mom—he's not really sick," Stevie said knowingly. "Just lovesick."

Mrs. Lake shrugged. The Saddle Club grinned at one another. Some things you just couldn't explain to a parent.

"Sure beats green hamburgers, Mom," Stevie said after a few mouthfuls. They had told Mrs. Lake about most of the day's events, including Chad's food-coloring ploy.

"I'm glad you like it, dear. Who knows? I might get

used to cooking and cleaning again—every few weeks or so," she teased, serving the girls second helpings.

After dinner they went upstairs to hang out in Stevie's room and rehash the past few days.

"What I can't believe," Carole began, "is that we really thought Max wouldn't be able to find someone for himself. How could we be that dumb?"

"I don't know, but all the women we invited sure made me feel lower than a snake," Stevie said.

"Tell me about it!" Carole said, already starting to giggle.

At the thought of the incident Stevie was referring to, the three of them burst out laughing and couldn't stop. One of the most memorable scenes of the whole day had come after the fireworks had ended. As everyone walked back to Pine Hollow together, the women had begun to thank the girls for inviting them to the picnic. Stevie had turned to the group and said, "Oh, you're welcome. I'm so glad you could all come. I'm just sorry it didn't work out with Max."

"What do you mean?" Nicole asked suspiciously.

"Yes, I thought he enjoyed giving us the talk, and a lot of us are planning to take a few lessons," Miss Cartwright put in.

Stevie bit her lip. Somehow she didn't think the truth would go over very well. But the women were staring at her, awaiting an explanation. "I just meant that it's too bad that Max had already—uh—met someone because we were kind of hoping—" She stopped, noticing thirteen pairs of flashing eyes.

"We were hoping that one of you might marry Max," Carole said succinctly.

Sergeant Kiernan stopped short. She put her hands on her hips and drew herself up to her full, highest-ranking-noncommissioned-officer-on-base height. "Carole Hanson, do you mean to tell me that you and your friends staged a manhunt, and we were supposed to chase after Max?"

Carole nodded reluctantly.

"It wasn't exactly a hunt," Lisa said defensively. "It was more of a—"

"A beauty contest?" Tiffani asked with a giggle. The women glared at her.

"A sort of an audition," Lisa finished.

"Well, I can't speak for the others, but I will tell you girls this: If you think I came here on this beautiful day to waste my time competing for some prize of a guy, then, honey, you have got another think coming."

At the end of Sergeant Kiernan's speech, the women had burst into applause.

Stevie reached across Lisa to grab a tissue from the box on the floor of her room. She wiped a tear from her eye. "The funniest part is," she began when she could stop laughing, "we would've said the exact same thing if anyone had tried to get us to go after some boy, but that never even crossed our minds."

"I know," Carole said. "I figured that if they found out what was going on, they'd be flattered to have been asked."

"One person was—Tiffani. I think she was hoping there would be a swimsuit and evening-gown competition following the picnic," Lisa joked.

As they talked, the girls changed into their sleepwear —a flowered nightgown for Lisa, striped pajamas for Carole, and an oversize rally T-shirt and shorts for Stevie. They weren't ready to sleep, but they wanted to continue talking in bed. They were about to get out the sleeping bags and pillows when the phone in Stevie's room rang.

"I hope it's not Phil," Stevie said. "I can't wait to tell him everything, but I'm too tired to describe today in detail again." She picked up the receiver and said, "Hello." After a second she mouthed, "It's Max." Carole and Lisa crowded around to try to hear what he was saying.

"Stevie," Max said gravely, "I have some unfortunate news to share with you."

"Yes?" Stevie asked nervously, her mind racing. Had Deborah left him again, but for good this time? Had the women been more upset about the picnic than they had acted? Had someone died of green-hamburger poisoning?

"When Deborah and I returned from Washington this evening, I got a call from Mr. Biddle," Max said.

Stevie let out a huge sigh of relief. She could easily work her way out of this. "Max, I can explain," she began, but Max cut her off.

"And I told Biddle that he ought to find better things to do with his time than yelling at three of the most gutsy, determined, clever, thoughtful girls I know." Max paused.

Stevie, Lisa, and Carole were speechless with delight.

"I heard all the details about the search-and-rescue team," he continued, "and all I can say, on behalf of Deborah and me, is thank you a hundred times."

Carole and Lisa began to swing each other gleefully around the room. Stevie searched for the appropriate answer to Max's thanks. She settled on the truth. "Max, there are some things a person has to do for himself—or herself. We really had nothing to do with it," she said.

"I'll never believe that for one second," Max said. "And we can't wait to thank you in person."

Stevie tried to protest, but Max would hear none of it.

"Max thinks I was just being modest for us," Stevie said after hanging up. "But I was telling the truth: There *are* some things people have to do for themselves."

With that she yanked open the closet door to get pillows for Carole and Lisa. Instead of her own usual mess, she saw two huge wicker baskets, one filled with dark laundry, the other with whites. Clipped to one of the baskets was a note, written in her mother's handwriting, with the heading: "Directions for washing and drying lights and darks."

At Stevie's groan Carole and Lisa came to her side and peered in.

"You know what?" Lisa said. "There are also some things that friends have to do together."

She picked up the dark load. Carole picked up the light load. Stevie grinned, grabbed the detergent, and set off down the stairs. They still had a lot to talk about, but the best thing about being part of The Saddle Club was that they could talk anywhere—Stevie's room, a stall at Pine Hollow, even the Lakes' laundry room!

About the Author

BONNIE BRYANT is the author of more than sixty books for young readers, including novelizations of movie hits such as *Teenage Mutant Ninja Turtles*® and *Honey, I Blew Up the Kid*, written under her married name, B. B. Hiller.

Ms. Bryant began writing The Saddle Club in 1986. Although she had done some riding before that, she intensified her studies then and found herself learning right along with her characters Stevie, Carole, and Lisa. She claims that they are all much better riders than she is.

Ms. Bryant was born and raised in New York City. She lives in Greenwich Village with her two sons.

We hope you enjoyed reading this book. If you would like to receive further information about available titles in the Bantam series, just write to the address below, with your name and address: Kim Prior, Bantam Books, 61–63 Uxbridge Road, Ealing, London W5 5SA.

If you live in Australia or New Zealand and would like more information about the series, please write to:

Sally Porter
Transworld Publishers
    (Australia) Pty Ltd
15–25 Helles Avenue
Moorebank
NSW 2170
AUSTRALIA

Kiri Martin
Transworld Publishers (NZ) Ltd
3 William Pickering Drive
Albany
Auckland
NEW ZEALAND

All Bantam and Young Adult books are available at your bookshop or newsagent, or can be ordered from the following address: Corgi/Bantam Books, Cash Sales Department, PO BOX 11, Falmouth, Cornwall TR10 9EN.

Please list the titles(s) you would like, and send together with a cheque or postal order to cover the cost of the book(s) plus postage and packing charges of £1.00 for one book, £1.50 for two books, and an additional 30p for each subsequent book ordered to a maximum of £3.00 for seven or more books.

(The above applies only to readers in the UK, and BFPO)

Overseas customers (including Eire), please allow £2.00 for postage and packing for the first book, an additional £1.00 for a second book, and 50p for each subsequent title ordered.